Undercover Temptations

Copyright

Disclaimer

The books in this series are based completely on dreams that I've had or that one of the other people in my relationship has had. They all have a little bit of real life thrown in so that you, the reader, can get to know us a little bit better.

These books can and should be read as standalone books. There isn't an order to them. All of the characters in the books are the same, as they are all based on characters from real life.

As you read these books, please keep in mind that other than the characters and the city they are based in, these books are not connected to other books in the series. They aren't a continuation of other books. They are all novellas based on dreams that revolve around the same characters.

As you keep that in mind, please enjoy reading this book. I do hope you will also read the others in this series and love them as much as I loved writing them!

Opening Quote

Steel to my trembling lips. How did the night ever get like this? One shot, and the whiskey goes down. Bottom of the bottle hits. Waking up my mind as I throw a fit. The breakin' is takin' me down. My heart's beating faster. I know what I'm after. I've been standing here my whole life. Everything I've seen twice. Now it's time I realized. It's spinning back around now. On this road I'm crawlin'. Save me 'cause I'm fallin'. Now I can't seem to breathe right. 'Cause I keep runnin' from my heart.

Runnin' by Adam Lambert

Chapter One

☆ DJ ☆

"Dad? Why is mom such a bitch?" my twelve-year-old son, Layne, asks as he sits down next to me. I keep my eyes closed as I lean my head against the back of the couch. I love my son, but it's been a long fucking day, and this isn't a conversation I want to be having.

What I want is to kick back with a cold beer and forget this day ever happened. If there was a reset button on life like there is on my PlayStation 5, I'd be all over it. I'd start everything about this day over. I'd call in sick and stay in bed. Seems like the best plan I've ever come up with. Too bad the Gods don't agree with giving humans the ability to turn back time.

I sigh long and hard. "Because it's in her nature, buddy. Good thing I have custody of you and not her, huh?"

I've never spoken truer words. Besides my son and family, I'm pretty sure nothing in my life has worked out the way I thought. I love my job. I love working with SWAT. I love being a Sergeant with the Gainesville Police Department. It's all I've wanted to do my entire life. I reached the goal, and I'm proud.

Ironic that it's a job I love so much that keeps me from being honest with not only myself, but everyone around me. At least part of the reason. The other part is I honestly question if my family and friends would still want anything to do with me if they knew who I truly am. This dark being that I keep shut away behind a façade.

To everyone who knows me, I'm nothing more than a good forty-nine-year-old guy who is a single father providing the life he never had for his son. I'm a good cop who tries his damnedest not to miss one of Layne's basketball games or softball games. I try not to miss holidays. Even if I'm working, I do my best to stop by a game or drop in on family dinners.

I go out on dates. I take time for myself. I make time to spend with friends. To everyone, I'm a regular guy who loves his family.

"She promised me she'd be at my game today. She wanted to make up for the last time."

I open my eyes and scrub my hands down my face. "She'll come up with an excuse for it. You know she will. I wish I could tell you that she'll change but it won't. I'm not going to lie to you about it, buddy. I hate that she gets your hopes up, though. Go get ready for bed."

"But it's not time for bed." Layne looks at me curiously. I glance over his shoulder at the wall clock. How the fuck is it not eight o'clock yet?

"Then go take a shower or bath or something."

He laughs "Dad, I did already."

I grin. "Then how about leaving me alone to wallow in my own self-pity for five fucking minutes."

Layne laughs again. "Why didn't you just tell me to go away and finish my homework?"

I raise an eyebrow. "You still have homework?"

"Well, no. I don't."

"Because you're too smart for your own good."

He smiles. "Bad day?"

I chuckle. "Kinda. Yeah."

"Maybe a shower would help."

I chuckle. "Maybe you're right."

Layne grins as he gets up. I follow him up the stairs as he heads for his bedroom. I walk to mine and take his advice. I take a shower. When I get out, I feel a little better. My son is very smart. It's probably why he's

6

skipped grades. He's in eighth grade this year. He'll be starting high school next year. An entire year early.

I throw a pair of sweats and a t-shirt on and walk to Layne's bedroom. I chuckle when I see him happily snuggled into his bed with a comic book.

"Hi, dad," he says, looking up at me. "Feel better?"

I lean against the door frame and fold my arms over my chest. "Yeah. I am. What comic are you reading tonight?"

"Batman."

I smile. "That's my favorite. Did you steal it from my room?"

He laughs. "No. You bought me it."

I chuckle. "One hour. Bedtime."

"Okay, dad." He curls back up with his comic as I head back down the stairs.

I yawn and head straight for the kitchen. I grab a beer from the fridge and begin walking outside to my back patio. I'm stopped in my tracks by a rather loud knocking on my door.

"I can't catch a fucking break today," I growl as I pivot and head for the door. I shake my head as I throw it open. "What?"

"That any damn way to answer the door for your best friend?"

My throat goes dry as I stand looking at my best friend, Matt Chance. He's a Lieutenant with Gainesville Police Department. He's just as tall as he is muscular. He's six feet four to my six feet three. His arms are covered in tattoos. His short dark hair is a mess, but the kind of mess that doesn't look like a mess at all. His eyes are dark and intense enough to feel as if they are burning through my own jade ones.

I clear my throat and take a drink, trying to cover up the fact that I was just staring at him, imagining everything I'd like to do to him. Beginning with my tongue down his throat. Him pushed against the wall with me pressed against every single one of his ridges.

Fucking hell.

"You intend on inviting me in? Florida is warm most of the time, but that wind whipping around out here is a little nippy."

I can't help but allow myself to drink him in as I step back. I take another swig of the beer as he steps inside. I don't know how the hell he makes jeans and a black leather jacket look that good, but he does it. Matt

7

fills out all of his clothes to perfection. His uniform. Jeans. Fuck. He even looks good in gym shorts.

I shake my head before thoughts of sweat dripping off his abs invade my head. Matt is the entire reason I get hard ons in the gym. Fuck. He's the entire reason I get hard ons at all. I bite back a groan as he takes his jacket off and hangs it up on one of my coat hooks. Why does all of his clothes have to look like they're painted on?

"What are you doing here at this hour?" I finally ask. Matt heads for my kitchen. He's managed to make my house feel like it's just as much his.

He bends over to grab a beer. I immediately snap my eyes away and take another drink. If I didn't know better, I'd swear he knows my secret, and every movement he makes is intentional. Like he knows what he does to me. Like he knows I'm gay and am head over fucking heels in love with him.

But there's no way he can know that. No one, but my other best friend, Lyric knows that. If anyone else did, I wouldn't have the respect I do at the department. Or maybe I would. The truth is, I don't know. If I'm being honest with myself, I'm afraid to find out.

Matt closes the refrigerator door and leans against the counter as he opens the bottle of beer. My son thinks I'm a superhero. My family thinks I'm brave. I run into situations others run away from.

But I'm not a superhero. I'm not brave. If I were, I'd be able to tell Matt how I feel. How I've felt for years. I'd be able to admit that one of the reason things didn't work out with Layne's mother is because I'm attracted to men.

It's something I've fought for as long as I can remember. For many years, all throughout high school when all my friends found the cheerleaders hot, I thought something was wrong with me. Because I didn't. I didn't find the popular, attractive girls in high school hot. I found the guys on my football team hot.

Matt's intense gaze seers into me. "I thought you could use some company after getting your ass reamed today."

I sigh and head for the patio. "Grab me another beer." I don't bother looking back at him as I walk outside and drop into a chair near my grill. Matt follows with another for us both. He drops down in the chair next to me. He's right. It's cold out here tonight. But I could care less.

8

"Well?"

I don't need to look to see he's looking at me. "Well what?"

"Don't be an asshole. You know what."

I look out over my backyard pool. The wind rustling the water, and the moon glinting off it makes it look like diamonds. Rough cut diamonds, but diamonds nonetheless. I take a long drink of my beer, finishing it off. I immediately open the other one.

"You know the accident wasn't my fault."

"I know. Doesn't mean the department doesn't need to investigate it."

"What's to investigate? I had my emergency lights on. I slowed down at the red light. She crashed into the back of my squad because she was texting and not paying attention. She admitted it. So what's to investigate?"

"Anything involving an accident with one of our officers is going to be investigated, DJ. You know that."

I take another drink, growling low in my throat as I glare at the water. "I do know that. Doesn't make it less irritating, though. Why should the department investigate me? I did everything right. I slowed for the red light to make sure no vehicles were coming. I didn't slam on my brakes. I had my lights on going to an emergency call for help. I couldn't do a damn thing about her crashing into me."

Matt puts his hand on my thigh. My eyes snap instantaneously to where his hand rests. Heat courses through my body and straight to my dick. I close my eyes and pray to any God that's listening to help me keep my dick in check. After a moment, I open my eyes and focus on the water.

"You know as well as I do what's going to come out of this. You haven't been suspended. But I had no choice but to send you home for the rest of the day. It's policy, DJ." He squeezes my thigh and looks out at the water.

I release the breath I didn't know I was holding as he lets go. I reach down to subtly adjust myself. Out of the corner of my eye, I see Matt catches me in the act. I'd be embarrassed, but I'm too fucking tired to give a shit, so I take another drink and keep my hand on my dick.

"I'm a good cop. That accident could have been what cost that woman her life today."

9

"And we finally get to the reason you're as upset as I can see you are."

I sigh because he's right. I had been on my way to a domestic disturbance when my squad was hit from behind by a woman who had been texting her boyfriend. She hadn't noticed the light had turned red, or that I had slowed down. I had to call another squad who was further away from the call than I was to take it. By the time he arrived, the woman had been stabbed twelve times. She died on the way to the hospital.

I look over at him. "I was almost there, Matt. I was three blocks away. That woman caused a three car accident that could have been totally avoided. I could have gotten there in time. I could've saved her life."

"Or... maybe not. I know how hard this is on you. I came over here tonight because after I interviewed the paramedics who got to that woman's house, the consensus is the same. It wouldn't have mattered if you hadn't gotten in that accident. She'd been stabbed while she was on the phone to dispatch. She was already on her last breath by the time they arrived. And they had been dispatched at the same time as you. The scene was already under control. The guy was already in the back of the squad when they got there. They didn't have to wait to get in the house. There was nothing you could have done, DJ. Nothing."

I search his eyes for a few moments looking for anything that would tell me he's only telling me something he knows will make me feel better. Seeing no deception on his part, I feel a little of the tension I've felt the past few hours dissipate. I lean back in the chair and let my head fall back as I swirl the beer in my bottle.

"I don't know if that makes me feel truly better or not."

"Losing someone on a call is never easy. You've been a cop for almost twenty-five years. You've lost a couple people. Wasn't easy on you then. Won't be now."

"This is different. I've never lost someone like this. I've lost people on medical calls. This was..." I shake my head. Matt puts his hand back on my thigh again and gives it another gentle squeeze.

I choke back a groan and try to hide my growing problem. It doesn't work, so I stand and down the rest of my bottle in a couple long swallows. I glance back at Matt, catching him watching me. I see his eyes flare with something I don't recognize. I quickly turn away, knowing that

I'm seeing things that aren't there. My emotions are all over the place today.

I walk back into my house and head straight for the kitchen. I contemplate another beer but remember Layne. I can't get wasted with him in the house. If something happened to him, and I couldn't do anything because I got drunk, it would kill me. I wouldn't be able to live with myself.

I opt for milk instead. I see Matt picking up my bottle I left on the ground outside as he grabs his and comes inside. He throws both of our empty ones away and opens his second one. I lean against the kitchen counter and hide behind my glass as I gulp the milk. Anything to keep my mind off him against my wall.

He leans against the counter next to me and sips his beer. "You do know I know you're gay."

I choke on my milk and stare at him wide-eyed. "What? I -" I cut myself off as he stares pointedly at my dick.

"I've known for a long time, DJ."

"How?" I shake my head. "I've been so careful. No one in my family even knows!"

"You think I don't recognize the signs of someone doing everything he can to hide who he truly is? Fuck, I've been doing it my whole life."

My mouth drops. "You're the object of every woman's fantasy that has ever come in contact with you. You flirt so well with them, they fall at your feet. I've known you for fifteen years. How the hell did I not know?"

He shrugs. "Too busy trying to deny it to yourself?" He grabs my glass. Good fucking thing because my hands are shaking so badly, I'd been dangerously close to dropping it. He puts the glass and his bottle by the sink, then he turns back to me. "I think maybe it's time you stop denying it." He puts his hands on the counter on each side of me as he moves closer until his chest is touching mine, and his lips are a breath away from mine. I suck in a breath as his dick presses against me. "Don't you?"

My heartbeat quickens. I can hear the beat in my ears like a bass drum. My eyes drop to his lips as he presses more firmly against me. I can feel his hard cock against mine. He grinds against it, and I feel like I'm going to bust out of my jeans. My hands grip the counter the closer he gets. I can't back away. I don't even want to.

11

"Fuck," I whisper. Before I can stop myself, I'm pushing off the counter and backing him against the very wall I envisioned him against only a little while ago.

My mouth crashes to his as his back hits the wall. We growl, moan, and groan into each other's mouths as our tongues fight for dominance of each other's. I know as soon as his hand finds my dick that I have no hope of winning the battle, though.

He backs me up to the couch, his hand squeezing my dick over my jeans. My hands are all over him like I'm a damn virgin. I don't know where to grab. I don't know where to touch. But I don't want him to stop for a second.

We both fall onto the couch. Matt doesn't let go of me. He continues his assault on my mouth as he undoes his jeans and mine faster than I've ever managed to undo a woman's bra. As soon as I feel his rough and calloused hand against the soft flesh of my hard as steel dick, I nearly come. I jerk into his hand as he strokes me hard and fast.

I look at him with dazed eyes as he pulls back from the kiss. He kisses down my jaw to my neck as he brings his dick against mine.

"Oh, fuck!" I arch against him as he thrusts against me stroking both of our dicks together tightly in his hand. I tug his hair as he bites my shoulder.

I feel him tremble against me as he pants against my neck just as hard as I am against his. We wildly thrust against each other. My dick throbs. I grip his wrist with my other hand as his mouth crashes to mine again.

"Fuck, DJ. Come for me. Now. Right fucking now."

I can't help but obey him. I come hard. I jerk and arch into him as I give him exactly what he demands. It's like my body is his to control. I have no say in the matter. His tongue meets mine in a fuck of tango as I moan. He moans low as he comes, soaking the front of my jeans and my cock as he collapses on top of me, his hips jerking to the same rhythm as mine.

My eyes slam open as I feel something wet hitting my face. I blink a few times trying to figure out where the fuck I am. I shake my head to clear the haze of just waking up from a deep sleep and realize that the wind is whipping rain against me. I look down when I feel something wet and see the front of my jeans soaked in come.

"What the hell? How did I even get out here?" The wind gusts and picks up one of Layne's pool toys, slamming it against the side of the house, cutting off any more thoughts I have about why I'm sleeping on my patio in one of the pool chairs. "Fuck!"

I stand up and run to quickly pick up the loose toys in the yard. I put them away in the shed and sprint back into the house as the rain starts pelting me, drenching my clothes. I start locking the doors and shutting off lights. I jog up the stairs as I strip off my soaked shirt. I check on Layne, satisfied he is sleeping. I quietly shut off his light and walk silently to my room. I strip off my wet clothing and hang everything to dry in my bathroom.

I don't bother getting dressed after I dry off. Instead I crawl into bed naked trying to catch my breath. Matt has been the object of my fucking fantasies for years. It's not the first dream I've had about him. I know very well it won't be the last.

I scrub my hands down my face with a groan. I'll never be able to tell him how I feel. Not only is he absolutely not gay, but I'd never want to ruin the friendship.

I roll over and bury my face in my pillows. I shake my head.

No.

Matt will have to remain a fantasy. Just like I will have to continue acting like one of Gainesville's most notorious playboys. It's the only way I can survive the shame I feel every single day at not being strong enough to tell everyone who I truly am.

Chapter Two

☆ Matt ☆

(Two Days Later)

I groan and lay my head back down on my desk. Attempting to put it up had been the biggest mistake I've ever made. My fingertips dig into the oak of my desk. I'd cry, but I won't let this hangover beat me. I'm stronger than that.

The knives being stabbed into every single part of my frontal lobe disagree with me. The world flips. For a moment, I question if I've somehow fallen out of my desk chair onto the floor and am really laying on my back staring up at the ceiling. I don't dare open my eyes to find out, though. That would be stupid, and I'm not stupid. A complete fucking idiot, maybe, but not stupid.

I groan again but don't move when someone knocks on my office door. "If you ain't toting a bottle and a half of Aspirin, go the fuck away," I growl. My own voice makes my head pound more. I briefly consider crawling underneath my desk and staying there. My door opens quietly. I squeeze my eyes shut against the lights from beyond the sanctity of the darkness my office provides. It shuts quickly. I send a silent thank you to whoever is responsible for making it happen fast.

"I don't have Aspirin, but I thought you might like to know that Captain McKay is looking for you," a sweet, very soft voice says. I can hear her sit, but opening my eyes is out of the question.

"Thank you for not turning on the lights, Mariah." I know I'm nearly whispering, but my voice is so loud to my ears that I begin praying for a quick death.

"Here. Try these. Better than Aspirin." She gently puts two gelcaps down by my arm as I victoriously open one eye without throwing up.

"What is it?"

"Excedrin. Only thing that works for me."

"Thank you." I slowly put them in my mouth and swallow them without anything to wash them down, then close my eyes again. I hear Mariah shuffling quietly before her small, soft hands start massaging the back of my neck. I whimper with pleasure, completely unashamed at showing weakness in my armor in front of her.

Mariah Carter is one of the best cops I have the pleasure of working with. She has this way about her. She walks into a room of chaos, and it almost instantly calms down. She puts everyone at ease with just her presence. But piss her off and she'll make a person regret the instant their parents thought of conceiving them.

It helps that she's beautiful. Long, gorgeous dark-brown hair. Wide, piercing blue eyes. Full lips. She's tiny. Maybe a couple of inches over five feet. She has a body any woman would kill for. Tits a man could drown in.

"If I weren't gay, I'd fall in love with you," I mumble as she digs her thumbs into each and every place that hurts, relieving pressure in my head with practiced ease. She's also the only person in this entire universe who knows I'm gay. Came out one day during her training. It's not my fucking fault the girl is so easy to talk to.

"You already are in love with me, Lieutenant. Everyone is." She says it as cockily as she possibly can.

I can't help but laugh. I wince a little at the pain, but Mariah continues to rub my neck and head. "Thing is, you don't know how right you actually are. Do you know how many guys I have to keep off you?"

"Too bad for them. I'm taken."

15

I smile a little. "How is Lyric? Enjoying her time off?"

Mariah laughs quietly. "Fuck no. She hates life right now. And she is not a fan that I make her sit with that foot up all day. She keeps saying the doctor gave her a walking cast so she can walk."

"In all fairness, she probably shouldn't have thought she could jump off my balcony into the damn pool."

"I don't think she realized the deepest end was only six feet."

"I don't know what the fuck demonic power possessed her and made her decide to jump in the first place."

"Well, you know Lyric. Sometimes she gets this weird little bug up her ass and goes slightly crazy. I'm surprised she hasn't tried to get me to jump out of a plane."

"I'm sure that's on her to-do list."

"There is no way in any universe I'm doing that. I hate flying. I hate falling even more."

She rubs the back of my neck a little more. I chance sitting up and leaning back in my chair. I slowly open my eyes. "What's McKay want?"

"Something about a case. He said he needs to speak with you and DJ before turnout and brief you about it."

"Do you think he'd let me get away with hiding in here all day and conference calling him?"

"Unlikely. This actually sounded like a pretty important case."

"I'm not getting out of this, am I?"

"Considering he pulled the Chief? I don't think so."

I groan as Mariah hits a particular spot on my neck right next to my ear that sends immediate relief to my entire head. "Fuck me. Where did you learn this? You've managed to relieve the pressure in my whole head in what? Five minutes?"

"You know I get nasty migraines, Matt. Lyric sometimes spends hours rubbing my head and neck like this."

"I might fall in love with her, too."

Mariah slowly stops rubbing and wraps her arms around my shoulders. "So? What brought this on? Heavy night of drinking?"

I sigh and glance at the clock on my computer screen as I reach up and grab her hand. I guide her to my lap and tug her down. Mariah is the only person I've been able to talk to about anything regarding my sexuality. She knows how difficult it's been for me to come out. I'm pretty

16

sure she's probably told Lyric. To Lyric's credit, she hasn't said a word, and I respect her all the more because of it.

I hug Mariah, anchoring myself. "That storm the other night ripped some of the shingles on my roof off. I had to fix it. It took a couple of days because I didn't want anyone to help. I wanted solitude on my days off. Last night, I decided to go out, and have a couple of drinks. Problem was a couple guys from the crew were there with their girls. I had already brushed off a few who had come onto me earlier in the night."

"Oh…" Mariah hugs me a little tighter, sensing I need it.

"In walks Sergeant DJ Asshole Rens with this gorgeous girl hanging all over him."

"Oh, Matt…"

I take a shuddering breath. "So, I left with the blonde who was practically riding me at the bar."

"I wish I could've helped you. Why didn't you call? Lyric and I would've gladly put on a show. Anything to take the attention off you so you could've slipped quietly out."

I shake my head in her hair and inhale her subtle coconut scent. It's one of the few things that manages to comfort me. Her and DJ's cologne. Though it's something I'd never admitted to anyone but Mariah.

"How the fuck did you manage to get me to soften and open up to you? I don't do that with anyone. But I'm so fucking comfortable with you and Lyric. Why?"

She shrugs. "Probably because you know we aren't judgemental." She pulls back and looks at me. "I still think you should tell DJ how you feel."

I laugh and shake my head as I nudge her off my lap. "Fuck no. What am I supposed to say? Hey, DJ. I know we're best friends and all, but I've had this crush on you for a long time. Care to come over and let me fuck you against the wall? See how far we can take this? Even though I know you're one hundred fucking percent not gay? Oh! And by the way. I know you've seen me all over women, but I'm gay."

Mariah laughs. "Sometimes, I think you're more dramatic than I am. And I can be seriously dramatic. But you haven't answered the question. What brought on the second worst headache I've ever seen on anyone?"

"Fuck, Mariah. Give me at least a little break, would you?"

17

"Pretty sure you know me better than that by now." She looks down at me with her hands on her hips.

I chuckle as I stand. I tower over her. How can such a little thing like her get me to open up the way I do? I'll never understand it. "When I got her home, I had to drink a lot more than usual to finish the job. Felt like shit about it, but I kept thinking of DJ and that girl. I guess I got a little pissed off, you know?"

She smiles softly as she looks up at me. "I... just... I have a feeling. And you've always trusted them before."

"I've trusted your instincts on the job before. I don't know about this feeling you have about DJ." I grab my service gun from my desk and put it in my holster. Mariah is adamant DJ is hiding who he really is just as I am. I'm fairly certain she's getting her signals crossed.

She sighs and smooths down my shirt. "You're so stubborn, Matt. Honestly. I don't know what to do with you half the time."

I smile. "You know I make your day better."

She laughs. "Yeah. You really do. I need to get changed. See you in the turnout room?"

"Yeah. I'll be there. If I don't get fired. The Chief being called into this meeting doesn't sound fun."

She shakes her head. "Why would you get fired? You're the best cop on the force."

"You have to say that. I'm your partner."

She starts walking towards my door. I follow and close it behind us as she smiles and chuckles. "You're just an incredible cop. You're an asset to the department."

"Always sucking up," I tease as I hug her. "I'll see you in there."

She smiles as she heads for the locker room. I take a deep breath and veer off the walkway to Captain Brody McKay's office as I rub my temples. I'm really not in the mood for whatever is in store for me today. Truthfully, I just want to avoid today and go home. I can't stomach seeing DJ knowing he was probably having the time of his life last night while I had to get so drunk I barely remembered my own name in order to get it up for long enough to please the woman who woke up wrapped around me.

I growl low and start to knock on the door, but it opens before my knuckles hit the wood. Standing in front of me is the six feet three inch

18

object of every wet dream I've had since I met him. I swallow hard and take an involuntary step back when I meet his eyes.

He grins. "I was just about to go see if you got lost. We sent Mariah to grab you a while ago."

I nod slightly trying to choke down the word vomit about to come from my mouth. I close my eyes a second before stepping around him into the office. "Fighting a headache."

DJ drops in the chair next to me in front of Brody's desk. "Fun night?"

I fight the urge to glare at him. Then fight the even stronger urge to puke. "Not really, DJ. No."

"Nothing pan out with the girl you had on your arm?"

I close my eyes against the jealousy creeping into every fiber of my being. After a few seconds, I open them again and settle into the cocky façade I've gotten so good at hiding behind. "It was fun. Not the best, but she did what I intended her to." I look over at him and shrug. "Satisfied the craving." I look back at Brody as something I can't discern crosses DJ's eyes. I refuse to allow myself to care. "What's up, Cap?"

Brody looks up from the stack of paper he'd been staring at. "We have a huge problem."

Our Chief sits on the edge of the desk. "There's been a few murders on the University's campus over the past couple of months. We've been able to keep it quiet as we investigate, but the media picked it up. It's… sensitive. And just became extremely high profile. We need to act."

I furrow my eyebrows together in confusion, trying to follow. "Isn't this the case you assigned to Lieutenant Brusche?"

"Something about an assault, right? You gave it to the Criminal Investigations Division," DJ says.

Brody and the Chief look at each other. Brody clears his throat. "We gave it to Brusche because of how sensitive it is. The problem is he hasn't gotten anywhere with it. We have no suspects. We have no motive. We have no witnesses. Nothing."

"Brody, I'm not understanding where you're going with this. Do you want me to take over the case? Because if this is something you want me on full time, then you need to get Mariah another partner. And I don't know how you're going to do that considering we're already short staffed and that being the reason I'm out on the streets instead of behind a desk where you want me to be anyway."

"That's not why we called you in here," the Chief says. "The reason we called you in here is because the shitstorm has started. Everyone wants to know why we're not doing anything to curb this. College kids are scared. Especially the young gay men."

I nearly choke. DJ starts coughing. I glance at him before focusing on Brody. He narrows his eyes and folds his arms over his chest as he leans back in his chair. The Chief stands and starts pacing. I shift uncomfortably, not liking where this is going. Judging from DJ's just as uncomfortable movements, I'd say he's right there with me.

DJ glances at me before looking up at the Chief. "What are you getting at?"

Brody stands and hands us each a file. "These are your new identities. First names remain the same. Last names change. You both are going undercover at the University. Your class schedules are in there. You've already been registered."

My mouth drops as I look at the folder in my hands. "What the fuck? Brody this isn't some fucking movie. You want to put me undercover as a college student? I'm almost forty!" I stand and drop the folder on his desk. "We have a fuck of a lot of younger guys who are just as capable of going undercover!"

DJ stands and looks like he's about to be sick. "You're asking us to pose as a gay couple according to that file. Why? Why us?"

Brody and the Chief look at each other. I instantly wonder if they know about me. Brody rubs his chin. "Because we know we can count on the two of you. You're a couple of our finest. This case is garnering a lot of media attention. There have been three murders. They've all been young gay men."

"The killer is targeting couples. He beats one of them up and leaves them to die. The other, he ties up, gags, and shoots execution style," the Chief says.

"We're asking the two of you to do this because you both fit the type of person he's going after. He's going after big guys. Muscular. Dark hair. Guys you wouldn't think would have a problem defending themselves."

20

DJ rubs his hands down his face. I can see the tension in his body. It's the same as I feel. He looks at them. "That's not a lot of information to go on."

"I know, DJ. But it's all we got," Brody says.

"We need your experience, and your expertise. Can you do it?" the Chief asks.

I meet DJ's eyes. They've turned into a dark pool of emotions. The same emotions coursing through my body. After a few long moments, I sigh. "Yeah. We need to end this. We'll do it."

DJ nods. "Yeah. Yeah, of course."

I barely hear any of the conversation that the Chief and Brody launch into. I hardly register the papers being handed to me. The instructions about going straight to the university after I pack up some things go in one of my buzzing ears and out the other. DJ and I in the same room. Together. Posing as a couple. One room. One bed to keep up the identity we're taking on.

All I can think about is the sudden pressure in my head that's come back with such force I feel like it may actually explode. I can't be in the same room with him. I can't live with him. He can't know how I feel about him. It would send him running away screaming from me. I'd rather have him in my life as nothing more than a friend than not have him in my life at all.

Fuck.

This can't be happening. It's like every force of fucking nature is against me. Like all the Gods in every corner of the universe are intent on watching me squirm and struggle. Because seeing DJ and having to fake having no feelings for him every time I see him isn't enough. Because being friends with him isn't me torturing myself on a daily basis.

I say nothing to anyone as the meeting ends. I take my file and flee the room. I avoid turnout, knowing Mariah is going to worry, but I can't bring myself to face anyone. Especially her and her totally fucked up way of reading everything I don't even know I'm feeling. I practically run for the sanctuary my truck offers.

I see DJ coming into the garage as I'm leaving. He's radiating so many different emotions that even though I'm in my truck and not really near him, I feel the waves of his intensity slamming into me. I avoid his gaze and quickly speed to the road heading home. I glance in the rear view mirror and take my first deep breath in I don't know how long.

I don't dare hope I'm right, but DJ looked like he was waging the same war that I am. There were so many things flashing across his chiseled face that seem to mirror my internal battle that I'm thrown into a state of utter bewilderment.

I know how I feel about him.

Is it possible he feels the same way about me?

Chapter Three

☆ DJ ☆

I slam my front door shut and lean my back against it, glaring into my house. Of all people to go on my first undercover assignment with, it has to be Lieutenant Matt Fucking Chance. And as gay college students, no less. Just because making me go undercover with him wasn't enough. No. We have to go ahead and seal the fucking deal with cement and throw it off a bridge.

Fucking hell. I take out my phone and dial Lyric, praying to Christ she picks up. "Come on, Lyric." I grip the phone tighter and close my eyes.

"Come on, Lyric? Really? Have you forgotten I'm crippled? Fuck. Like I can just run to the bedroom and grab my ringing phone just to appease you and your need to speak with me." Her voice is filled with so much sass that I have to smile. I called the right person.

Lyric is my partner on the streets. I miss her out there since her injury. Her presence constantly put me in a better mood. Which, lately, has been admittedly getting worse and worse. I don't know how she manages to make things better, but she does. It's probably her bubbly personality. Makes her the perfect compliment to my surly one.

23

"You know, we'd be the perfect couple if we weren't two flaming homosexuals." I smile as I open my eyes.

She laughs so hard she snorts. "No we wouldn't. We'd kill each other after the first date. You put on your big boy panties and tell Matt how you feel yet?"

"Fuck you. Why the hell do you ask me that every single day knowing full well what I'm going to say?"

"Maybe because I'm really, really smart. And one day you're going to be brave and take the chance like I did with Mariah. Then you'll be happy instead of this asshole you've turned out to be."

I groan. "I called you so you could make me feel better with that Lyric whatchamacallit you have. Not so you could remind me how miserable my life is, and what an asshole I am for allowing it to be like this."

"Fine, fine. Ruin all my fun. I'll stop busting your balls. What's up?"

"I'm getting put undercover."

"Well... Isn't that a good thing? I thought that was something you wanted to try out. Despite it meaning you'd have to leave Layne for a bit of time."

"I love Layne, but this would be a vacation. Lately, I think all he wants is to annoy me until he kills me."

"You may be the only man who thinks going undercover is a vacation."

"You haven't been around Layne the last three weeks."

"I miss them."

"Yeah? How about you take him? I'll have my mom help. Bring him to school and drop them off. You and Mariah can spoil him even more rotten than he already is."

"I don't mind. I can talk to Mariah. When are you going undercover? What's the assignment? Can you say?"

"Probably not. But I trust you and Mariah. There's been some murders on the campus. Young gay men. Couples."

"Oh... My... God..." She inhales sharply. I push myself off the door and head up to my room to start packing. I know I don't need to say more than that. She'll get the irony right away.

"With Matt."

24

"That... can't... be a coincidence. Can it?"

I shrug as I enter my bedroom. "Either Captain McKay and Chief know my little secret, or the Gods, both ancient and present, all had a meeting and are conspiring against me."

"I don't know whether to laugh right now or cry for you."

"Cry, Lyric. The answer is cry. This is going to be pure fucking torture. The only reason I'm going through with this is because I have this stupid need to help people. Apparently, it's a required quality to become a cop. And then it becomes a pain in the ass because suddenly you're being thrown into situations like this with people you're trying to avoid."

"Avoid? Get over yourself. You know as well as I do that part of you is ecstatic that you're being thrown into this with Matt. First of all, you can't think of a better person to do this with. The fact that you have an insane attraction to him aside, Matt is the best person for the job. He's your best friend. You trust him. And second, this is a huge opportunity for you. This is the type of case that can get you promoted. You've wanted to move up the ranks for a long time."

I sit on the edge of my bed with a long sigh. "Fuck me. How do I get thrown into these types of situations? I... this... can't come out. Lyric, you're the only one who knows about me. No one else does. Not my family. None of my other friends. It's..." I rub my forehead and lay back on the bed staring up at the ceiling. "It's not the same for men coming out as it is for women. There's such a stigma around it."

"DJ... You think there isn't for us? People are always asking us which one is the man. Who is on the top. Which one of us is the protector. We get called dykes. Just the other day, Mariah opened her locker to find an image of a naked man with a drawing of a giant penis. It's not that easy for us out there."

"Wait. She what? Why the fuck didn't I know about that? I'm one of her commanding officers!"

"Because Mariah doesn't let it get to her. She forces herself to treat it as a joke. Hell, so do I. Because if we didn't, we'd probably kick the fucker's asses."

I growl low and shake my head. I've always been protective of Lyric. Ever since I met her, there was just something about her that I was drawn to. She started a couple years ago with Gainesville Police

Department. She was in the same training class as Mariah. They hit it off immediately.

Ironically, I found that while I liked both of them right away, Lyric had been the one I'd become closest with. I'd always thought it was sort of perfect that Matt had become close to Mariah. Almost like we've become this inseparable group of friends that were destined to be.

I've always known they dealt with some type of harassment. I've disciplined officers they've reported. One of the newer guys slapped Lyric on the ass. He'd been fired shortly after for several more incidents specifically targeted at both Lyric and Mariah. Inappropriate images in the locker room of two women sucking a guy's dick. So many more images that took me completely by surprise.

"Lyric, I know what it's like for you. But for guys? I'd lose more respect than you could ever dream. Guys in this profession are viewed as weak. Less capable of doing this job than a woman. You know very well the shit some of the guys think about working with any of the women on the force. You know how much shit women take in that locker room."

"Yeah. I do. But we prove them wrong every day. Maybe you need to start doing that. You say you'll lose respect. Well, that may be true. But I bet you will gain just as much as you lose, if not more. You know your record. You know how good you are. You have the numbers to back you up. You have to prove to them how strong you are. And if they give you shit, throw your record in their face. And the stripes you wear on your arm."

I shut my mouth because I know she's right. I can't argue with her. I'm one of the best cops on the force. I made Sergeant within a couple of years of being hired. I do my job, and I do it well. If I'm being honest with myself, I'm running out of excuses to not come out. Truth is, I'm just scared. I'm scared of the reaction I'll get.

I let out a long breath and close my eyes. "What do I do, Lyric? I'm supposed to pretend like I'm a young man head over heels in love with Matt."

"Well… you are…"

"I know. Well not the young part. I'm fucking fifty. That's another stupid thing about this entire situation. But how am I supposed to portray I'm in love with him in public, then shove it all back down behind closed doors? According to the file, we've been given a one bedroom dorm. That means one bed. One bedroom. One bathroom."

"So?"

I sit up shaking my head. Tears sting my eyes. "I can't do this."

"Okay. DJ. You know how I feel about being all… dominant. I feel weird. But you have to hear this. You're going to stop being a scared little boy. You are going to get your ass to the University. You're going to do this with Matt. Because above everything else, he's your best friend. People are depending on you to help them and solve this case. And you are going to pay attention to Matt and his reactions to you. Because I've said this so many times to you. I really think there's something you're missing with him. Now get your ass off your bed and get moving. I want to see my nephew."

Lyric hangs up before I have a chance to say anything. I have to laugh because it's very Lyric. Not letting me get a word in edgewise when she knows she's right. I shake my head and stand to finish packing.

After making arrangements with my mother to help with Layne, I call Lyric again as I jump in my black Ford Mustang. I head towards the University with my millionth low growl of the day.

"You know, you should stop calling me when you're making all these sexy growls," Lyric says when she answers.

I laugh. "Too bad you'll never get to enjoy them."

"My entire reason for being is to get you out of your thick skull long enough to laugh a little. What's up, Rens?"

"I'm on my way out. Can you and Mariah just stay at my house? It's easier than moving Layne around."

"Yeah. I already talked to her. She said she'll be done early so we can head over there. I'm just packing things."

"Be careful on that ankle," I chuckle. "What the fuck ever made you decide to jump from Matt's balcony into his pool anyway?"

"It looked like fun."

I shake my head. "Just… it looked like fun?"

"It was hot. The pool looked inviting. Why walk all the way down the stairs when there's a perfectly good balcony overlooking it?"

I laugh. "Fuck. You have got to have a death wish. I've never even done that."

"I wouldn't call it a death wish. More like a fun streak."

27

I laugh again. "Fine. Fun streak. When are you going to be at my house? Need to let mom know."

"Um... it's looking like dinner. By that time, I expect your tongue to be down Matt's throat." She laughs. "Or your lips wrapped around his dick. Either way works."

I groan as my dick immediately hardens at the thought. I reach down and rub it as it throbs. "I hate you."

"No. You love me because you know I speak the truth. Have fun, DJ!" She hangs up on me. Again.

I squeeze my dick a couple of times to relieve the pressure as I shake my head and throw my phone on the seat next to me. When I get to the University, I stay in my car for a few minutes with my head back against the seat allowing the cool air to relax me. I gulp in several deep breaths.

I know Lyric is right. I'll do this because it's my job. Because I love my job. Because there are people who need help right now, and I'm one of the only ones who can do it. They're counting on me to ease their fears. To protect them from this bullshit. To find the person responsible for punishing them just for who they are.

Thinking about the case puts me in the mindframe I need to be. I get out of my car and start grabbing my stuff. I've never understood serial killers. I guess I've never understood why someone would feel the overwhelming need to kill someone in general. But serial killers. What the fuck kind of person do you have to be to target a certain group of people just based on particular qualities? Like how they look. Or what color hair they have. Or if they are gay or attend a particular church. I've even seen people targeted based on where they are employed.

I start heading into the dorm building with my stuff. I'm hoping I get there before Matt so I can at least adjust to everything before he invades. But as I open the door, I realize I'm not that lucky. Matt is grunting as he installs the wall mount for a large TV. His muscles in his arms and back bulge as he drills in one of the screws.

I forget how to breathe.

"Why are you not wearing a shirt?" I blurt before I can stop myself. All I can see is the beads of sweat dripping down his back. And think of how badly I'd like to lick them all off.

28

"Because it's ninety degrees, and I haven't set up the window air conditioner yet." He finishes the wall mount and turns. His jeans hang low over his hips. I have to close off thoughts of ripping them off to get to the prize underneath.

"Why is there no A/C in here already set up?"

"Are you going to come in here? Or stand there fucking gawking all day? It's not a fucking resort."

I step in and close the door. His tone immediately irritates me. I drop my stuff. "A/C is mandatory. Isn't it?"

"We're undercover, DJ. The University didn't rent this room to actual students because there's shit wrong with it. They didn't have the budget to fix it. Heating and cooling unit is broken. There was also leaky gas. They had it shut off. The department paid to have it fixed so we could get in here."

"Tell them to pay to have the fucking A/C fixed," I grumble as I look around.

It's smaller than a typical one bedroom apartment. The walls are a dim beige. Kitchen is small. It's an open floor plan. The hallway that leads to what I assume is the bathroom and bedroom is fairly narrow and not that long.

"We're lucky we got in here at all." Matt turns and grabs the TV. "Make yourself useful and help me with this. Might want to lose the shirt. We have a lot of work to do if we expect to make this at least tolerable."

I shake my head as I walk over to him. "I'm fine."

"Don't say I didn't warn you. Hold this so I can mount it."

I do what I'm told, but it's not easy. Matt's cologne is intoxicating and overpowers everything else. The grunts and low growls he's making are enough to make me envision what they would sound like with him underneath me or on top of me. Or in every creative position I've invented in all of my fantasies.

After a couple of hours of moving things and some cops in plain clothes delivering furniture and a bed, I'm stripping off my drenched shirt and wiping sweat off my forehead. I pant a little and kneel next to the window to catch my breath.

"Fuck, we need to get that window A/C in right now. It's two hundred fucking degrees in here," I growl.

29

"It's in the bedroom. I have another one coming. Should be here soon. Mariah is bringing it on her way home."

"She's going to pick Lyric up and head to my house."

"They staying with Layne?"

"Yeah. My mom didn't seem too happy when I said I didn't know how long I'd be. Lyric was fucking ecstatic."

Matt's smile could brighten any room and mood. "She might love that kid more than you."

I laugh as I stand. "She's my go-to when he's driving me crazy, and I need a break."

"And I'm sure you get him back hyped up and sugar-crazed."

I smile. "Actually, no. You'd think so with Lyric's sweets cravings. But he comes back well-behaved. He loves spending time with them."

Matt tosses me a bottle of blessedly cold water. We both drink them down in only a few long swallows. After a couple more minutes, we get back to work setting up our bed in the closet of a bedroom. Our king-sized bed gives us very little room to move around. Our small dressers double as nightstands. The closet in the bedroom barely holds both of our clothing.

By the time we get to the bathroom, we both end up washing up with the ice cold water before we can attempt to make sure everything is clean and ready for use. I find myself praying Mariah shows up with the other A/C unit because Matt and I are so hot that we've decided we're staying in the bedroom.

Laying on our backs looking up at the ceiling next to him is about as tortuous as being pushed into a volcano. I close my eyes because I can't look at him. My resolve to not jump him has become precariously thin.

We need to figure out sleeping arrangements. There's no way in Hell I can lay next to him in this bed like he had suggested as we were setting it up.

Adults.

Friends.

Capable of being mature.

Fuck all of that. When it comes to Matt, all I want to do is lose all of my control. Unfortunately, I barely have any control left. I'm terrified of knowing what will happen if I allow myself to lose that last tiny, thin thread.

Chapter Four

☆ Matt ☆

I collapse on the couch hours after I showed up at the dorm. I close my eyes and allow the cool air flowing into the room to calm the raging flames of desire that the heat and DJ shirtless has managed to cause within me. I don't know how I'm going to get through this. Not knowing how long this case is going to take is pissing me off. Not having a plan is pissing me off. DJ sitting next to me is pissing me off. The sound of the fan in the A/C unit is pissing me off. Everything is pissing me off.

"We should go grab something to eat. We need to get groceries. We can go to Walmart. It's open."

I groan. "Have something delivered. We can go tomorrow."

"As much as I'd like to say yes to that, no. Tomorrow we start school. That means a day filled with classes and… whatever the hell else college kids do."

"At least our classes are the same. I haven't taken a college course in seventeen years."

"Let's go. We should at least get a little bit of a feel. Make an appearance."

I growl deep in my throat as I get up. DJ has changed into black jeans and a light blue t-shirt. Why and how he manages to look so damn good in whatever he happens to throw on is something I have yet to understand. His dark hair would look unruly to most. But to me? Perfect. He's fucking perfect.

"Fine." I quickly stand up and stride to the bedroom to change into something less sweaty.

I'd agree to just about anything if it meant getting away from him and his cologne. I don't know what it is, but it's been the scent that's haunted my dreams since he walked into my life. It's something strong. Musky. But there's an undertone of something sweet and fresh. Earthy. Comforting. As soon as it hits me, I feel instantly relaxed.

And I hate every second of it. I hate that of all people in this universe that could be my soulmate, it has to be DJ. Why it couldn't be someone gay, I absolutely don't get. Obviously God never liked me. Which is just fine with me. I was always more comfortable at Satan's side anyway. As Mariah would say, it's so much more fun to be bad.

After changing, I meet DJ in the living room and take a moment to look around. If I'm being honest, we did a damn good job. The small, one bedroom dorm looks comfortable and lived in. Like it belongs to a couple in love. Some of both of our things are intermingled together, creating a nice fusion of the two of us. The dorm room is very much me and DJ. As much as I want to deny it, I fucking love it.

"We should take a few pictures of us together," I say as I grab my keys. "Grab some frames, and get them up. Only thing that's missing."

"Yeah. I agree." DJ takes a last look around before following me out. We nod at a couple of students on the way to the door of the dorm building and start walking towards one of the nearest restaurants. "What are you in the mood for? Pizza or burgers?"

I look around at the choices as we walk and notice that we're drawing attention from a few people who noticed us moving in. A couple new guys starting classes in the middle of the semester is bound to get people talking.

Which is what we want.

I sigh and take DJ's hand. Every blood cell in my body is immediately alight. "We need to make it look real."

DJ squeezes my hand and links our fingers. "I know." We walk in silence a few moments before DJ clears his throat. "Burgers?"

"I could go for something greasy after all of that shit."

"That was a lot. We deserve a little treat."

"Want to take it to go and eat it outside by the dorms? It would give us time to observe."

"Yeah. We can do that."

A few minutes later, DJ and I walk out of the restaurant and start heading back to the dorm. DJ takes my hand as I carry the bag with our dinner. When we get back to the building, DJ sits. I sit next to him and start handing him his food.

"Do you think we're going to be able to figure this out?" I ask. Doubts of my own skills nag at me the more I think about what little we have to go on. I don't even know where to start. It's so unusual for me that I shiver.

"We make a hell of a team. I think we have a good chance, at least. I've already looked up some LGBTQ clubs on campus. When they have meetings and get togethers. There's one for gay men that meets tomorrow night in the Southwest Recreation Center."

I smile softly to myself. "Your skills never really cease to amaze me. I feel out of depth here, but there you are... researching and thinking of things I hadn't."

"That's what makes us such a great team." He shrugs and rests his leg against mine as we eat in comfortable silence.

I focus on the contact and let the heat and comfort that it brings move its way through me, soothing all of my tension and uncertainty as it goes. I may never be able to have DJ, but I can revel in moments like this to keep me going.

(Two Days Later)

DJ and I hang near the back of the crowd as we watch the rally happening in front of us. We've heard about these rally's on campus. We've done security work for them. Being involved with them, though, is

34

something else entirely. The happiness and excitement radiating off every person in the Quad is something I've never experienced. The group is so welcoming of everyone that it's impossible not to feel like I've become one of the students. Even though it's only been a couple of days since DJ and I showed up on campus and interjected ourselves into the group.

They keep saying that it's a safe zone. That everyone is free to be themselves with them. And it's the truth. Everyone is comfortable. Everyone seems to feel secure. There isn't a single person here who hasn't let loose.

"It's different being on the inside than it is on the outside making sure everyone is safe," DJ says in my ear, referring to the police officers guarding the perimeter of the quad the rally is being held in tonight.

Last year's rally, those officers were me and DJ. I'd never admit it, but even then I wanted to be a part of this. Experience it as someone who didn't need to hide who he truly is or who he loves. Let go like everyone here is right now.

"Still have to be on guard, though," I say back to him. "Make sure nothing is off."

"We can have a little fun in the meantime. We're supposed to be undercover, afterall." He elbows me with a wink before taking my hand and dragging me into the crowd.

Before I have any time to react, DJ is dancing to the beat of the song one of our local bands is playing. I can't keep up because all I can focus on, all I see, is DJ. Every bump against me makes me hum. Every touch sends shockwaves through me. He's so close. Chest to chest. His lips are dangerously brushing my skin.

"Fuck me," I whisper low enough that he'd never be able to hear it over the music or the loud crowd.

"Need to loosen up, Matt. Ain't going to work any other way. We need to look like a couple in love." His breath against my ear makes me forget about the crowd. It's like they vanish around me.

I grip his hips and turn my face into his neck, resting my lips against his skin. I pull him tightly into me with a groan. His arms automatically find their way to my shoulders. I grind against him hard, not giving a shit who sees.

"You want this to look real? Okay." I crush my lips to his, holding him against me. I have no more resolve. No more fucks to give.

35

I can't resist it anymore. I don't even care to. I've wanted this for too long and far too much to even attempt to stop. I'm sure I'll face backlash, but I'm too weak to resist this any longer. I expect him to push me away. I have no doubt he'll tell me it's too far.

But he doesn't.

To my utter astonishment, DJ pulls me impossibly closer and plunges his tongue into my mouth. He meets mine in a frenzied fight for dominance while he grinds himself just as hard against me as I had been against him.

If I thought I had been hard before, I was wrong. My dick damn near rips through my jeans as soon as I feel his solid length against me. I unabashedly slide my hands down and grip his ass with a possessive and ferocious growl. We're going to need to talk about this. Because now that I've tasted him, there's no fucking way I can go back.

DJ's fingers grip my t-shirt. His nails dig into my shoulders as we continue grinding against each other. He sends electric sparks through me when he bites my lip with his own possessive growl as his hands move down to grip my ass. He squeezes, and it's all it takes for me to start searching for a place we can be alone. If I don't have him in a far more intimate position soon, I'm going to end up coming in my jeans.

I don't have the chance to start tugging him to a dark corner, though. He beats me to it. Holding my hand tightly, DJ drags me behind a building nearby. There's no one around and we can't be seen from any direction. He's just as smart as I am. Even though no one can see us, we can see if anyone is coming up on us.

DJ drops to his knees in the grass and pushes me against the brick wall. I bite my lip when he sucks me in his mouth seconds later. It takes me a few moments of clearing the haze to realize he just unzipped my jeans and pulled my dick out.

I grip his hair and choke back the loud moan that threatens to escape when his tongue finds and hits every single place on my tip that makes not coming impossible. He pumps my dick slowly and firmly in his hand. He takes me further and further into his warm, wet mouth, not stopping his strokes for a second.

"Holy shit, DJ," I whisper as I quietly moan. I don't know if I'm dreaming. If I am, I don't want to wake up.

36

"I've waited fucking forever for you." DJ twists his wrist, quickening his pace and continuing to stroke firmly.

His other hand finds and tugs my balls. I choke back a scream of pleasure and tug his hair. He scrapes his teeth along my length and sucks hard just below my tip before taking me back into his mouth. Slowly. Inch by glorious fucking inch. My vision blurs as soon as I touch the back of his throat. He swallows around me with a low moan.

I can't hold back. I come harder than I've ever come in my life. I come so quickly that I don't have any time to warn him or even try to pull him off. I gush hot liquid down his throat as he swallows every fucking drop like it's the greatest thing he's ever tasted. He licks and sucks me clean as I collapse against the bricks.

"Fuck. Oh, fuck," I pant as he packs me away and stands. He kisses me again as he presses my large and still semi-hard cock against my thigh and zips my jeans. I taste myself on his tongue, but all I want is to taste him.

As usual, though, luck is not on my side. We quickly pull apart when we hear voices coming our way, but stay near enough to each other, holding one another's hand, as we listen. It sounds like a lot of people who don't sound all that happy about there being a rally for the LGBTQ community. DJ and I stand close to each other.

"Problem is the university caters to the little queers," a deep male voice says.

"Ain't shit we can do about it," another says.

"Well, that ain't totally true. Someone sure is doing something about it," still another says.

There is a chorus of laughter as they come around the corner. DJ and I sink further back, though we can see the crowd now. There's several of them. I do a quick count. Eight. All big guys. All wearing basketball jerseys.

"I don't know who it is taking them out, but I'd sure like to shake his hand," the first guy who spoke says.

"There's this guy in my theater class," another guy says. The crowd stops near us. "Dude is fucking scary. Big guy. Wears all black. Looks like a goth, but he's far fucking scarier. He's quiet as hell. He was writing something in his notebook last week. It was a description of

37

someone. Nothing else. The very next night, a guy is murdered that matches the description he's writing down."

DJ looks at me as he shifts uncomfortably. Neither of us want to be anywhere near these guys, but we both know that any information we can get that leads us to the serial killer we're after is good information. We turn back to them as they start walking again. Directly towards us. I quickly look around and tug DJ. Time to make an escape.

"Well, well, well... What do we have here? Two little queers hiding out?"

I swallow hard. All of my instincts scream danger. I've never run away from a fight, but even I'm not stupid enough to stick around when the red flags start going up. I don't bother turning around as I continue tugging DJ with me. We need to get back to the safety of the crowd. At least to the safety of the cops around guarding the rally.

But yet again, God decides to play a cruel fucking game. The eight guys surround us, leaving us no way to escape. I glance at DJ. We both are armed. We both have guns strapped to our ankles. The problem is getting to them before the guys surrounding us reach us.

DJ lets go of my hand and slowly holds his out as he raises them to about his shoulders. "It's okay. Stay calm. What seems to be the problem here?"

I follow his lead, keeping my eyes on the crowd. "We're just minding our own business here. We don't want any trouble."

"Well, that's just too damn bad," the guy with the deep voice says. I've quickly decided he's the leader. Probably the Captain of the team. "Because I'm really itching to teach you fuckers a lesson about equality. I'm so sick of all you gay little boys and girls getting everything you want handed to you on a silver fucking platter."

Out of nowhere, I'm hit in the back of the head so hard that I fly forward directly into the arms of the leader. I have no chance of defending myself because before I know what's happening, I'm on the ground fighting through blinding, stabbing pain shooting from the base of my neck all through my head.

I haphazardly attempt to fend off kicks and punches that I can't see coming at me. I cover my head, feeling like it's the only thing I can do to survive the blows. I curl my legs into my stomach and make myself as small as a man who is six feet four possibly can. I try to look for DJ, but

38

every time I turn my head or try, I'm taking another blow to my arms and chest and back.

Just as quickly as it starts, it's over. DJ is leaning over me gently pushing my arms back while he barks orders at people. Footsteps and scurrying fill my ringing ears. My heart is pounding so fast that I'm not convinced I'm truly breathing.

"Stay with me, Matt," DJ says. He's somehow managed to pull my head onto his lap.

I don't know how long I lay there before I'm calm enough to dare move. I take a deep breath as the thunder rolling in my head finally stops. The dizziness I didn't know I had been experiencing suddenly vanishes.

I start to sit up but groan when the dizziness hits me full force. "Fuck," I mumble into his thigh.

"Don't get up, baby. Ambulance is on the way."

All I can do is nod and close my eyes. "What the fuck happened?"

"They all went after you. All of them. I was shoved away and held back by one of them, but I got free. I started hitting and kicking and shoving everyone off you. Cops nearby heard the commotion. Came running."

I moan quietly as he runs his fingers through my hair. "I didn't have any time to react."

"I know. Fuck, Matt, I'm sorry. So fucking sorry. Don't talk. Please."

I grip his shirt and cough into his thigh as he gently rocks me back and forth. Even through the pain I feel in every bone in my body, I've never in my life felt so safe. Usually, I'm the one defending others.

But right now, all I want to do is bury myself in the protection I feel coming off DJ in waves. I don't want to let myself feel the vulnerability that's trying to steal its way into my mind.

All I want is him.

Chapter Five

☆ DJ ☆

Sometimes, I wonder if I'm crazy. I wanted to be a cop for as long as I can remember. Who the hell actually wants to be a cop? It's a thankless job filled with dangerous situations. We just may be the most hated profession in the entire world.

What makes me crazy is that I've never questioned it. I have Layne at home. A son I sometimes wonder if I'm going to end up leaving fatherless. I've been shot at. I've been on calls that scared the ever living fuck out of me. Still, I've *never* questioned it. Not one single time have I ever questioned it.

Until today.

Watching Matt lay as still as a statue on the hospital bed makes me question everything. If we weren't cops, he wouldn't be here. He'd be safe. He'd be at home sound asleep. He wouldn't have bruises all over his body. He wouldn't be hooked up to an IV. He wouldn't have taken the beating he did because we wouldn't have been there.

I rub my thumb across the top of his hand and watch the machines clicking and monitoring him. I keep looking at my watch while I run my fingers through his soft, dark hair. We've been here for over three hours. I called Lyric and Mariah, but neither answered. I really hadn't expected them to. It was one in the morning when I called.

The doctors had given Matt morphine for the pain. Nothing was broken, shockingly, but he has bruised ribs to go along with the massive amount of bruising everywhere else. Thankfully, nothing internal. He'd been going in and out of a deep sleep since they added the morphine to his IV.

I reach up and wipe my eyes for the thousandth time. I look down when he squeezes my hand. Our fingers have been linked like this ever since I fought off his attackers. Part of me is afraid to let go for fear I'll lose him.

"They come back with the tests yet?" Matt asks weakly.

I look up at him, fighting back more tears. "No. Not yet. They said as soon as they know, we'll know."

Matt winces as he nods and shifts. He squeezes my hand tighter. "Did you get a hold of Lyric or Mariah?"

I shake my head. "Texted. Left twelve voicemails. I think they both silenced their phones last night."

"Rih never does that."

"Then she's out like a damn light because she didn't answer."

I keep running my fingers through his hair as he blinks a few times. He yawns and turns his head towards the window before turning it towards me. He reaches for the button on his bed to raise it a little as he squeezes my hand once more.

"Thank you. For everything. I don't really know all you did, but I do know I was caught off guard. I wouldn't have survived if not for you. I've never felt so fucking weak. That's never happened to me before."

I close my eyes against the dam about to break again as I shake my head. "You would've done the same."

He reaches up and runs his thumb over my lower lip. I open my eyes. He cups my chin. "I've been wanting to tell you something for a while now."

I lean into his touch. "It can wait. You... just need to get through this."

He slowly drops his hand but keeps his eyes on me. "I've been in complete love with you for far longer than I care to admit, DJ. I'm sorry it took this long for me to say anything."

41

I smile a little, though my heart stops beating. "It's the drugs talking, Matt. And probably the alcohol we were drinking at the rally."

He chuckles and shakes his head. "I had one beer. It wasn't alcohol that had either of our tongues down each other's throats. And it wasn't alcohol that had you sucking me off behind a building. I guess I didn't realize that you felt the same way. Considering you're with a different woman every other night."

I can only stare at him as he closes his eyes and situates himself, sitting up a little further. "I…" I shake my head and look down at our hands. I don't dare hope any of this is real. I look back at him. His beautiful brown eyes meet mine. "I'm not the only one who went home with a gorgeous woman more times than I can count."

He smiles weakly. "Truth is, DJ, I was afraid to admit it. I don't know what the fuck made me kiss you the way I did at the rally, but I do know now that it was the right thing to do."

"How can you say that?" My heart breaks at the words I'm about to say. "How can you sit there and say that us finally admitting that we're very obviously gay and attracted to each other was the best thing? Matt, all of my fucking fears came true! My feelings for you put you in the hospital. Feelings I still haven't fully admitted to having!" My mind races in so many different directions that I can't keep up.

Matt sits up with a low groan and cups my cheek. I don't know how he does it, but I'm instantly centered. My heart calms. My racing thoughts slow. His hand slowly moves around to the back of my neck. He pulls me towards him. Our lips meet in a fiery explosion of passion, yet the softest and sweetest kiss that I've ever felt. The type of kiss a person needs but doesn't know they need.

Matt pulls slowly away but keeps me close to him as he looks at me. "I get the fear. I get the stigma. But I also don't give a shit. I've gone far too long hiding. I should've taken Mariah's advice a long time ago and just told you. But I didn't because I didn't want to lose you as a friend. I would rather only be friends with you than be nothing to you. And I was afraid of how people would react. But you know what? The couple days have been the most real I've been with myself in a long time. I'm not going back. We're going to finish this. And we're going to figure out where we stand. I'm not going to lose you. Not after finally having you. Understand me?"

42

I swallow. I'm terrified to lose him more than I am at admitting how I feel, but I know hiding is futile. I wouldn't be able to go back to the way things were before if I tried. Now that I've given in to every single desire I have, there's no way I can give him up.

"I'm scared, Matt. For more reasons than I think I really even understand." I look at him a second before taking a deep breath and dropping my head gently on his shoulder. "But you're right. I should've taken Lyric's advice and told you a long time ago. She kept saying that she feels like there's more that I don't know. And now I know that if you've been talking to Mariah, then she was right." I chuckle. "I don't know what I'm supposed to say or feel or how this goes, but I've…" I take a deep breath. "I've been in love with you for a long, long time."

He reaches up and runs his fingers through my hair. "I gathered that. When you said you've been waiting a long time for me right before you sucked me off."

I can't help but laugh as I look up at him. "Where do we go from here? How does this even work?"

He shrugs. "Aren't we always telling Lyric and Mariah that love is love? Doesn't really matter what people think. It's about us. Not them."

"What about Layne? Our family? Jobs?" I know I'm letting all of my uncertainties get in the way of the happiness I should be feeling.

"We'll take it all as it comes."

We both jump a little when the door to Matt's room flies open. I turn to see a frantic Mariah and wild-eyed Lyric flying into the room. They both surround Matt. Mariah doesn't hesitate at all to climb into the bed with him.

"Are you okay?" Lyric whimpers, sitting on the bed next to him.

"I'm okay. Bruises, but I'm okay. Really." He hugs Mariah because she's given him no choice. She's burrowed into his side as she cries quietly. Matt still hasn't let go of my hand.

"What happened? Who did this?" Lyric asks, searching my eyes.

"I think a few guys on the basketball team. They were all caught. Cops at the rally converged pretty fucking quickly. We were lucky." I look back at Matt. "Really fucking lucky."

He smiles and kisses Mariah's forehead. "DJ swooped in and saved the day."

43

Lyric leans forward and hugs Matt before damn near launching at me. "I'm so happy you both are okay."

"And finally together," Matt says.

Lyric pulls back with wide eyes. "What?" She looks between the two of us as Mariah raises her head to wipe her eyes. "Like… for real?"

"For real," I say quietly.

"How?" Mariah whispers.

I glance down at Matt. "We were checking out the rally. Trying to blend in. I guess one thing just led to another. I told him we need to make it look real. Next thing I know he has his tongue down my throat. That was it. I knew right then I couldn't hide my feelings for him anymore."

"Then he dragged me behind a building and got me off in less than a minute."

Mariah's eyes go wide as Lyric giggles. Mariah slowly sits up. "In public?"

I shrug. "It was a heat of the moment thing."

"I'm shocked," Lyric laughs. "Totally shocked that it escalated like that. I thought you two would talk after being stuck in a dorm together."

"We had a bet going. She thought you'd talk. I thought Matt would have you against a wall within a day or two."

I smile at Mariah. "Guess you both lost."

"With epic proportions," Lyric says as she rolls her eyes. "So, how did this happen?" She gestures to Matt.

"We heard some voices," Matt starts. "We stayed quiet. We could see them, but they couldn't see us. They were throwing around a bunch of bullshit homophobic insults about the rally. They started talking about the murders."

"They were talking about how they were all for them. One of them said if he met the murderer he'd shake his hand. They started walking towards us, so we very quickly walked away. Before either of us knew what happened, they had us surrounded. Next thing I know, Matt's getting a beat down. One of them had me by the neck. I got away pretty quickly and threw him into his little gang. I just wildly started punching and hitting. Anything to get them off him."

"Cops guarding the rally got there pretty fast. I could hear them but didn't know what the hell was happening. DJ barked a few orders out. It probably all happened in less than a minute, but I was attacked so quickly from behind that I had no time to react."

"All I care about is that they were all arrested. Matt's okay. We're just waiting on a few test results. They'll probably release him as soon as we get them. Unless something is wrong, but they already said they think he's good to go. Just going to be sore."

"They'll never find those poopfilledassmunchers bodies if I ever get my hands on them," Lyric grumbles.

I chuckle. "Down girl. From what I've been told, they've all been booked into jail and charged with assault and hate crimes."

"Well," Mariah chuckles. "Their college careers are nice and ruined."

"Serves them right." Lyric looks at Matt. Her eyes are full of concern, but she doesn't get the chance to say anything. Matt's doctor walks in.

After a few minutes of discussing his results, being assured that he's okay, then reassuring both Lyric and Mariah that the doctor wasn't lying, I hand Matt his jeans. Lyric and Mariah both reluctantly left, but not before forcing us both to promise we would check in. Like we wouldn't check in with them anyway. The two are honestly our best friends. They've become like our family. There's no way we wouldn't check in with them.

I watch Matt closely as he gets dressed. When I'm satisfied he isn't going to keel over on me, I help him make sure he has everything before we start leaving. It's only then I realize we don't have a vehicle here.

"Fuck," I say as I scrub my hands over my face. "I need to call a Lyft." I start taking out my phone.

Matt grabs my wrist. "You mean that one?"

I look up at the car pulling up in front of us and smile. "Still watching my back."

"Damn right."

I chuckle as I open the door and help him in. I climb in next to him as he winces. "You doing alright?"

"Everything fucking hurts. I want a long shower and bed. Then I want to regroup and figure this thing out."

I look at him incredulously. "Fuck, are you kidding me? We aren't going back in."

He smiles and looks over at me. "Yes we are. This is fucking personal now."

I shake my head. "You can't be serious."

He rests his hand on my thigh but says nothing. I open my mouth to argue more, but he squeezes my thigh and shoots me a look of warning before his eyes flick to the driver. I close my mouth with a low growl, but I say nothing. Neither of us say a word until I close the door to our bedroom in our dorm room.

"DJ, you know we have to finish this."

"The department can find two others to throw in here! You're hurt! Our cover is going to be blown the second the D.A. calls us to the witness stand!"

Matt sits calmly on the end of the bed and looks up at me. "We'll fill out affidavits. There's ways to work around cops who are undercover."

"Yeah! They're called witnesses! We don't have any!" I frustratedly scrub my hands down my face before looking at him again.

"DJ." He watches me as I pace. I put my hands against the wall and face away from him. I tense as I push off it. "DJ. Look at me."

His calm, deep voice pisses me off, yet soothes me. I turn around and look at him. "You were attacked, Matt. We both were. That makes us targets."

"But we're trained to handle it. Wouldn't you rather an assailant come after you than a defenseless individual without the amount of training and expertise you have?"

I look up at the ceiling and close my eyes a moment before I open them and look back at him. "You know the answer to that."

"This guy is targeting guys like us. Guys just living their lives. Minding their own business. Not doing anything wrong. The only difference is that they don't have the defensive or the offensive skills we do. They don't have the training." He grips the waistband of my jeans and tugs me to him, positioning me between his legs. "Isn't it our responsibility to stop the fucker? Do our part to keep the community we ourselves are a part of safe?" He rests his chin against my rock hard abs and looks up at me as he locks his arms around my waist.

I sigh and run my fingers through his hair as I look down at him. "I'm terrified, but you're right." I look out the small window as the sun rises over the campus outside the relative safety of the walls we've

46

surrounded ourselves with. "But I feel like you're a target now. Like we both are." I look down at him. "I don't know how to feel about that."

He smiles as he pulls back slowly. He starts to unbutton my jeans. I suck in a breath. "Scared. You'd be stupid as fuck not to be." He keeps focused entirely on my jeans as he unzips them. "Maybe slightly exhilarated. Kind of like we always are before a SWAT call." He pushes down my jeans with my black boxer briefs. My already hard and larger than average size cock flicks out. "But you know what we have to do."

He lowers his mouth and gives my dick a long, slow lick. I tug his hair and moan. "Fuck…"

He smiles and closes his eyes as he takes my tip in his mouth. He slowly starts pumping my dick as he sucks my tip. His tongue swirls around in a circle. He does something with his mouth that has my knees buckling and me questioning my own name. He scrapes his teeth along the vein that runs along my cock as he tugs my balls before going back to firmly stroking.

He slowly takes me further into his mouth. I close my eyes and let myself feel all of the warmth and wetness his mouth offers. He starts rolling my balls around with one hand while he strokes faster with the other, matching the pace he's sucking and licking as he bobs his head up and down along my dick.

He starts sucking harder, taking me further and further into his mouth. When I touch the back of his throat, he swallows and hums low around me sending vibrations straight through my dick, making me harder than I've ever been in my life. He repeats the motions again and again, still stroking me and massaging my balls in his large hands.

My fingers tangle in his hair. I tug harder. "Fuck, Matt. Don't fucking stop."

"Wasn't planning to." He rotates his wrist as he strokes and starts tugging my balls hard as he gently rolls them in his hand.

"Fuck!" I push my dick into his mouth until I'm touching the back of his throat again. He rewards me by swallowing and humming low once more. It's all it takes for me to come. Hard. I throw my head back as he drinks me down like I'm the last drop of water on Earth.

After I finish, Matt sucks and licks me clean. "You're right. It was worth the wait." He looks up at me teasingly. I groan and lean down, kissing him hard. After I pull back, he looks back up at me, locking his arms back around my waist. "I'm going to take that shower."

I nod. "I'll... get everything ready for bed. Make sure we're locked up and shit."

I step back as Matt gets up. While he takes his shower, I throw both of our clothes in the small washing machine we weren't aware dorms on campus had in the rooms. I quickly do the dishes and pick up the few things we've left scattered around. A t-shirt over the chair. My hoodie on the couch. By the time I hear the shower shut off, I'm just finishing up. I check the door, making sure it's both locked and bolted shut, before I walk back to the bedroom.

I close the door and turn to the bed. Matt is already laying down on top of the blankets asleep. Completely naked.

"Fuck," I whisper to myself. I allow myself to take in his incredibly perfect body. He takes care of himself. Just like I do. He's toned. Fit. He looks a little like he's been chiseled from granite. His ridges and lines are... hard. Like him.

I force my eyes away and head for the shower. I quickly take mine, not wanting to leave Matt alone for any longer than I have to. When I'm done, I follow his lead and climb into the bed next to him just as naked as he is. I pull the blanket we have folded at the bottom of the bed up and around us. For the first time in longer than I can remember, I fall into a peaceful and deep sleep wrapped around the one person I've never questioned wanting or loving.

Despite everything that we're up against; everything I'm sure we're about to face, I finally feel like my life is how it should be. It's perfect.

Chapter Six

☆ Matt ☆

(Two Weeks Later)

Normally when I take a woman on a date, I find the most expensive restaurant in town and show off. Expensive wine. Expensive bill. My truck isn't an option for picking up a woman for a date. It's too tall. So I rent a car. Usually a convertible.

Expensive.

It's never been about more than one date. The date has always been for the sake of keeping up appearances. I knew that I'd never go past the first one. I knew that I'd never take things further than one night. But I always made sure the woman I was with was treated like a Queen.

And it's that particular thing that kept women flocking to me. My reputation typically preceded me when it came to the women I chose to go out with. They knew they'd be treated like royalty and have a fun night. And none of them expected anything more.

It suited me just fine because I only ever needed them to make me look good. To keep me hidden behind the smoke and mirrors I created for myself. I was deemed a playboy. Second only to maybe DJ.

49

But I was okay with that. It meant that DJ hadn't fallen in love. Some sick part of me kept thinking that just maybe I'd have a chance with him. It also meant that I was safe. No one knew the secret.

I'd never been nervous about it. I'd never been nervous planning a date. I'd never been nervous about footing an expensive bill. I've never even really been nervous about the conversation. Or the end of the night.

Things at the end of the night had become increasingly harder, though. I wasn't really sure how much more I could take. The longer I talked about things with Mariah, the more I started understanding that not being true to myself is making me miserable. And being miserable isn't healthy for anyone.

I know how lucky I got with DJ. Not everyone ends up with the person they feel such a strong connection with. Especially when that person is gay and the person he pines for appears not to be. I honestly felt that even if I quit hiding, I'd still be miserable. I've never wanted another man the way I do DJ.

Which brings me to the nonsense of tonight. I've been pouring over restaurants in the area that would get us exposure, but this is mine and DJ's first date. I want it to be perfect. I've never cared about a date being perfect. But this one, even though we're going for this case, I want it to be perfect. Though fuck if I know why.

DJ has never been one to care about flashy cars and expensive dates. He's never given a crap about wine and cost. DJ has always been content with box wine and Pabst Blue Ribbon. He'd be content hiding in a campground for a week. Or renting a boat and getting lost. I could probably just go to the local burger joint and get takeout. We could eat it right here on the couch and watch a game. DJ is very low maintenance.

Doesn't mean I don't want to make the night as special as I can for him. And going to the pizza parlor or taproom isn't something on my list of special things. I have to do a little better than that. I wouldn't be able to live with myself otherwise.

"Maybe I should just take him to Disney or Universal," I mumble. "He loves those amusement park rides." I shake my head. "Fuck. This is fucking ridiculous."

"What's ridiculous?" DJ asks as he comes around the corner, buttoning his jeans.

50

I lick my lips as my eyes go directly to his dick. I snap my eyes back up with a small chuckle. "Nothing. I was just trying to find a restaurant for tonight."

"Why not just hit that pool bar?"

I smile softly and shake my head. "Seriously. I called that. But I thought things could be a little… I don't know. Maybe a little more special?"

DJ slides my laptop aside and sits on the coffee table in front of me. He takes my hands in his and looks at me. "Matt. I don't need the fancy bullshit you're used to doing on dates. Give me a beer and a pizza. I'm good. All I want is you. I don't need any of it. I don't need to worry about Layne. I know he loves you. And he's really the only one I care about, other than my mom. Now that we're really together and doing this, I guess to me everything else just seems…" he shrugs. "Unimportant? I don't care about the looks or judgements anymore. I'm tired of all of it. Now that I have you, everything else just doesn't matter."

"If I didn't know any better, I'd think that my ice heart is melting," I tease.

He leans in and kisses me. Deep and long. The kind of kiss that brings out an unexpected moan and makes me instantly hard. DJ moans right back and deepens the kiss. Our tongues clash in a frenzy of sparks and electricity that should send us both flying backwards and writhing on the ground.

Instead, I tug DJ closer. I shift and both tug and pull him to the couch. I barely hold back a full on pounce. I crawl on top of him and kiss him again just as deeply. He wraps his legs around my waist and pulls me against him as he sucks on my tongue. I spear his hair and tug, kissing down to his throat as I push my dick hard into his.

"Oh, fuck, Matt." He arches and tilts his neck to give me more access. I bite it lightly with a low moan when he rubs against my dick with his again and digs his nails into my back.

"Fucking hell, DJ. I'm about to bust through my jeans."

"Me, too." His teeth scrape across my shoulder, and I grind into him.

I know if I don't stop soon, this is going to go further than either of us might be ready for. I force myself to slow down, though I'm not totally sure I want to. I kiss him deeply and slowly.

I pull back slowly. "I think we might want to stop before we end up not leaving this dorm."

He chuckles dangerously as he grabs my dick. "Would that really be such a bad thing?"

I let out something suspiciously like a whimper. My dick seems to hum in his hands. "Fuck, DJ. Have you ever actually been with a man before?"

He looks at me and lets go slowly. "No."

I smile and lean in and kiss him again. "Me either. But I think we need to ease into it."

He smiles as he slowly sits up. "I'm ready. If that's what you're worried about."

"Oh, baby, it's not about being ready. I just want to do things right. I don't want this to be sex and only sex."

He leans in and kisses me. "To be continued. I don't want to wait much longer for you. I'm too fucking old for that shit."

I chuckle. "I don't either. But I still want to do it right. We're just now admitting feelings for each other. Jumping into bed just seems too fast."

"You don't need to explain it. I understand." He kisses me again. I can't help but smile. "But still. To be continued. We've spent how many years fighting the attraction between us? We know who we are. We know what we want."

I laugh. "Got it. Trust me. I don't want to wait. But I think we at least need a date. And finish this fucking case."

"I'm not fucking waiting until the case is done." He gets up and leans in kissing me hard. I bite his lip as he pulls away. "I don't think I can. I've never wanted anything more than you."

I groan as we both adjust ourselves. "So where do you want to go? And would you please actually pick a place? I'm not talking about a taproom or pool hall."

"Why? That's where all the kids are."

"Because... I said so. That's why."

He raises an eyebrow. "Okay. Fine. There's a pizza place around here. It has sit down seating, and a nice... ambiance." He waves his hand in the air so adorably that I laugh. "Not too stuffy. Not too casual. Want to try that?"

I smile. "Yes. A happy medium. I'm okay with that."

"I've seen a lot of college kids there, too. So we can still make ourselves known. Observe. See what kind of info we can dig up."

"Okay. Good. Then can we go? Because if you aren't going to do something about my hard on, at least feed me."

He smirks as he heads for the door. "You're the one who stopped me, asshole."

I follow, laughing. "For reasons."

A few minutes later, DJ and I are being seated in the pizza parlor. The hostess leaves quickly to grab our drinks. I lean into the table and reach across it for DJ's hands. He takes them, and we rest them on the unnaturally pure white tablecloth spread over the hardwood table. The glass bowl in front of us has a real tea-light floating on the top of the crystal clear water. There's a soft scent I can't quite place surrounding us. Calming.

DJ smiles and brings our hands to his lips. He kisses them softly as he looks at me. I can't help but smile back and fall a little deeper into his jade eyes. I never realized how truly beautiful they are. I've always thought they were a dark brown or something, but really, they're jade. Deep jade.

"I still can't believe this is happening," I say. "It seems surreal."

"It's the way it was always meant to be. I truly believe that. I guess I can't say I'm not a little scared about reactions from... well... everyone. But this. You. This is how my life was meant to be."

I look up as our server walks up to the table. He's a slightly scrawny man. His sandy blonde hair is greasy and unkempt. He wears a pair of thick, black framed glasses. His clothes are hanging off his body, leading me to believe the guy probably hasn't seen a gym in... ever. I haven't let go of DJ's hands. I'm slowly rubbing my thumb across the tops of them as we look up at the server.

He glares down at us. "What do you want?"

I can feel DJ's hand jerk nervously, but I hold it tighter, keeping my eyes on the server. "We'll take a large barbecue ranch pizza with olive oil on the crust. And an order of gourmet cheese bread. We'll also take a bottle of the house wine."

The server's eyes zero in on our hands. "Sure. Anything for our community's elite." He rolls his eyes and heads back for the kitchen.

DJ lets out a long breath. "What the fuck was that all about?"

"Ignorance. Ignore it."

"I know it exists. I thought I'd prepared for it. I was wrong."

I bring his hands up to my lips and kiss them softly. "Ignore him. It's about us tonight."

"You're right. You're right." He shakes his head. "I'm too old to let some young college kid's opinion affect my mood."

"He doesn't matter. We're not here for him." I kiss his hands again then look back at him.

He squeezes my hands as he smiles. "Do you think we're going to catch this fucker?" He keeps his voice low so no one hears us.

"They did put us here. We're good at what we do. We'll catch him. It's what we're here for."

He smiles teasingly. "I thought we were here for us."

I laugh. "Right. Here for us. On campus for that. Now, would you just enjoy this? I'm trying to fucking lavish you with affection here."

"By all means. Continue lavishing." He laughs with me and kisses my hands as the server comes back to our table with our garlic bread.

He drops it hard enough to make the next table look over. "You know. There's a killer on the loose. Targeting gay men. Do you guys not look at the news or read a paper? I'd think you'd be hiding."

His sneer pisses me off. I slowly let go of DJ's hands and lean back in my chair as I return his glare with an intense one of my own. "What does that mean? We can't go out as a couple?"

"I wouldn't if I were being targeted. Seems pretty stupid."

"We're just a normal couple having a normal dinner." DJ leans back in his chair.

"Normal? Normal is the couple behind me. You both aren't a normal couple. You're just a couple of faggots."

I can feel my fingers clench into a fist before I can stop them. "And you have a problem?" I growl low.

"The whole restaurant has a problem with it. No one wants to see two guys all over each other."

"Excuse me, but none of us have a problem with it," a young girl says at a table near us. She shoots fire from her piercing blue eyes and immediately reminds me of Lyric as she stands. "Does anyone in here have any problem with these two young men showing their love and affection

54

for each other in no more of an in your face way than I have been with my boyfriend? They've been holding hands and lovingly kissing. Anyone?"

DJ and I stare at her in shock and awe. I barely hear the chorus of no's throughout the restaurant. My attention is on the server, and his suddenly very red face. But it's not embarrassment. He's seething. He's so angry his whole body seems to be vibrating with rage.

Moments later, the manager comes to our table and escorts our server to the back. The entire restaurant erupts in laughter and applause. Including the two men in the corner booth who are sitting shoulder to shoulder. They both give us a smile and nod.

"Well, that was fun," DJ says with a chuckle.

"I'm in disbelief that happened."

"It's like all of my nightmares came true, but it was so utterly entertaining that I almost don't care that it happened at all."

"I'm sorry to interrupt," the woman who spoke up says next to us. We both look up at her. "That just really made me mad. I hope you know that no one has a problem with you in the restaurant. So many men and women couples come in here. And there really are so many regulars."

"You both do you! Don't let anyone tell you that you can't," an elderly man who has to be in his eighties says.

"Bigotry and hatred will not be tolerated here," the manager says, appearing next to us. "We will not turn you away. And I won't let my staff talk to anyone like that. I would say I'd retrain him, but that seems stupid. He should know better. He's an adult. He's been fired."

"Oh." I shake my head a little surprised. "I didn't expect that to come out of this." I glance at DJ as the woman squeezes his shoulder and goes back to her table.

"I didn't either. I really don't know what to say," DJ says.

"No need to say anything. We hope you still feel welcome here. I'll make sure your pizza is out shortly. And your meal is on the house."

"Oh, no. Sir. Really. That's not necessary," I vigorously decline.

The manager squeezes my shoulder. "We take care of our customers here. I won't have it any other way."

A few minutes later, DJ and I have our pizza in front of us. We dig in with gusto, suddenly famished. We drink the bottle of wine and enjoy each other's company. We laugh and talk long into the night.

It isn't until we notice that the staff is starting to remove table cloths and put chairs on tables that we realize how late it's gotten.

"Shit. We've been sitting here for six hours," DJ says with a sexy smile. "I guess time flies when you're with someone you love."

My eyes widen. "Love?"

He nods as he looks at me. "I'm not ashamed to say it. I've felt like this for a long time. I'm old enough to know how I feel. It's not like it's instant love. I've been in love with you a long fucking time. I don't expect you to say it back, Matt. But I do love you."

"I feel the same," I say quietly. "I guess I just didn't want to say it so soon and scare you off."

He reaches over and brushes his fingertips along my cheek leaving a trail of warmth behind that goes directly to my dick. I can't take any more. I leave a very large tip on the table that covers not only our bill we were told we didn't have to pay, but also leaves the server that took over a very nice little bonus for the night. I take DJ's hand and lead him quickly out of the restaurant.

He laughs. "Little eager?"

"I crave you, DJ. I want all of you. I refuse to fuck you right now, but I'm going to take some serious pleasure in fucking your mouth."

"Fuck."

He squeezes my hand and adjusts himself as we quickly walk back to our dorm. Before I even get the door closed, we're all over each other. We strip each other's clothes and leave a trail on the way to the bedroom.

We fall into the bed in a tangled mess. Before I can even make the command or direct him to my dick, DJ has me in his mouth. He bobs his head up and down my length at the same furious pace I'm thrusting into his mouth.

I don't know how long it lasts, but when I come down his throat, I'm sweating, writhing and damn near screaming his name. DJ has a hoover of a mouth and knows exactly what to do to make me come harder than I've come for anyone.

Neither of us bother with a shower. Instead, DJ wraps his arm around my waist and pulls me into his side. I rest my head on his shoulder. We both hold each other tightly as we fall into a deep sleep.

For the first time in my life I feel like I'm where I belong. I feel completely happy with the person wrapped around me.

56

I feel content.

Chapter Seven

☆ DJ ☆

"What the fuck do you mean there was another murder?" I practically yell into my phone. I sit up in bed as Matt starts to wake up. I put the phone on speaker.

"Just what I said. Last night. They were found this morning," Brody says to me.

"Same motive?"

"Same motive. They were found with one bound and gagged. He was shot in the back of the head. The other was beaten to death. Bound and gagged just like his partner. Naked."

"Same mark?"

"Same mark. Three sixes on the base above their penis."

"Fuck." I run my fingers through my hair. "How the fuck is this happening? We have no clues at all. No information. No one is talking about this. No one knows anything."

"Even that guy the basketball team pointed out? The dark, scary fucking dude?"

"He's not scary at all. The guy is quiet," Matt says as he sits up, yawning. "He dresses in black. Has lots of tats and piercings. Comes off intimidating because he doesn't like people. He wants to keep them away. If that's a recipe for a serial killer then look at me. I must have over a hundred murders under my belt by now."

I chuckle. "What he's trying to say in his Matt way is that he's not our guy. We've both sat and talked to him. Matt's practically become his best friend. We've asked him a lot of questions about what's going on. There's just nothing indicating that our instincts about him are off."

"I trust your instincts. It's the reason you both were handpicked. But we have to find out something. Anything."

"We'll look into it, Cap," Matt says.

"We need something, Matt. Anything. This is six."

"We know, Brody. We'll figure it out." I hang up the phone and toss it as I lay back down on the bed and close my eyes. "This guy is good. There's no trail. How is this even possible?"

Matt lays down next to me and props his head up on his arm as he looks at me. "He's not better than us. Did Brody email the file for the last murder?"

"Yeah. I haven't looked yet." I close my eyes as Matt's hand is suddenly gripping my dick. He squeezes firmly and strokes at an even pace. "Oh… fuck."

"It occurred to me that you had me buried deep in your mouth last night, and I never returned the favor." He twists his wrist.

I moan and arch into his hand. "Fuck." I tangle my fingers in his hair and push him down towards my throbbing cock. He, thankfully, takes me in his mouth without making me beg. Which is a very good thing because I've never begged for a fucking thing in my life.

He moans as he bobs his head up and down. He continues stroking me firmly as he rotates his wrist. He's managed to hit a rhythm that isn't too slow or too fast. It's perfect. It has me arching and moaning and thrusting up into his mouth as he sucks and licks.

His teeth scrape lightly up the vein running along my dick, and my tip literally feels like it's on fire. My dick jerks. Like it has a mind of its own. My eyes roll back in my head at the feeling, but I have no time to savor it because the feeling shoots all the way down my shaft directly into my stomach. It tightens just as an electrical current jolts down my spine and directly to my dick. I feel like I'm going to come so hard I'll end up choking him if he swallows.

59

I tug on his hair. "Matt, fuck. Matt… I'm going to come."

"Mmhmm…" He licks and nips my tip continuing to stroke my dick.

I weakly try to pull him back, but all I can feel and concentrate on is the pulsing and throbbing of my cock. My hips jerk uncontrollably, and my head drops back on the bed. My fingers tighten in his hair. My dick touches the back of his throat. He swallows at the same time he tugs on my rock hard balls. My stomach tightens and spasms. My back tingles and tenses. I start shooting my come deep down the back of his throat. I arch and grip anything I can to keep from flying to dangerous heights, but it's no use.

Matt pulls back, slowly licking my dick as I finish coming. I pant. "Holy… fuck…"

He kisses my tip and crawls back up to me. He kisses me hard and deeply with a low moan. His tongue meets mine. I let him take total control of the kiss as I wrap my arms around him. I suck lightly on his lower lip as he pulls back.

"Now. Ready to do this?"

I blink at him, slightly dazed and a little unsure what exactly he means. Though, if it's his dick buried in my ass or mine in his, I'm all for it. I shake my head to rid the thoughts before my cock rebels and gets hard as fuck again.

"Do… what exactly?"

Matt gives me a quick peck before he gets out of bed. "We need to look over files."

I groan. "This case is pissing me off. Hardcore."

"Then let's get out there and solve it."

I sigh and get up. An hour later on a fucking Saturday, I'm sitting next to Matt on the couch in our dorm pouring over case files and images that would make anyone throw up non-stop until they're dead.

I shake my head and grab the pencil from behind my ear. I put images of the bodies on the table in front of me and start looking for similarities. Maybe then I can pick out anything else that stands out. I glance over at Matt. He's reading through reports and piecing together similarities of the scenes that are in the reports.

Once I have all of the similarities in the photos circled, I stare at each one individually. Positioning. Same. Marking on each body. Same.

60

The angle of the etching in the skin. Same. It appears to be the same room. Like the guy is bringing the bodies to the same place. A hideout? Maybe a warehouse.

"Hmm… Matt?" I ask as I eye the photos.

"Yeah?"

"The bodies. Where are they found? Are they all in the same area?"

"Science building. Basement. There's a private entrance to the basement on the East side of the building. The university has a keypad lock on the door."

"So… this guy has to have access. There's no way he could lure people down there without being seen if he went through the building. Too many cameras. Do we have a camera on the door?"

"We do. Last night there was an eight hour period of time where it looks like the feed had been cut. Surveillance didn't notice because the feed never actually went down. It just showed the back door. There was fifteen minutes that was looped to play over and over again. It just showed the door and the back area of the building."

"We only have one camera out there?"

"It covers the whole area. Surveillance didn't think they needed another one."

"So this guy has access to the Science Building. And he knows about our cameras."

"He's smart. He knows he's being watched."

"We need more cameras up."

"We need guys out there watching."

"Yeah. That won't get approved."

"I thought about more cameras. The problem is I think he has cameras up. I think he saw when we set ours up."

I lean back. "Shit. You're probably right."

He smiles but doesn't look at me. "Usually am. Finish looking through those. We need something to go on. We can't go to Brody with nothing."

I lean forward. Blood spatter is pretty much the same. "I don't get this. He cleans up after we leave the scene? He has to because the old blood spatter isn't on the walls."

61

"The university still has to function. Students use that basement. As soon as we clear the scene, they can do whatever they want with it."

"Is there a way we can get Brody to let us in?" I tilt my head as I grab one of the images.

"Why?"

"Because of this. It's not in the other images." I point to a broiler. Underneath it just barely peeking out is some kind of a card or white piece of paper.

"Holy shit." Matt starts flipping rapidly through reports until he gets to the one he needs. He scans it quickly. "It's not on the evidence log. Nothing was picked up in that area." He flips through more images and more reports and documents. "No. It's not here. Whatever that is, it was missed."

I pick up my phone to call Brody. "How the fuck was that missed?" For the first time in the couple of weeks we've been on this case, I'm truly excited. "This might be our big fucking break."

"What break? What did you find?" Brody asks when he answers.

"We found something by the broiler at the crime scene. It's too far away. We can't tell what it is. Matt pulled it up on the laptop. He's zooming in now, but it's blurry. Looks like paper or a card or something."

"Highlight it. I'll send it to tech. They can clean it up. I'll send Crime Scene down to grab it. Location is still secure. Tell me if you see anything else."

"We'll let you know." I hang up and lean into Matt as he goes through the images on the laptop.

"Nice catch."

"I wish I could tell what it was."

"Did you see anything else?"

"No, but I don't understand why the university is allowing the area to still be used."

"Actually, I was looking at that. It looks like the room is still locked down. The university has blocked it off to students. You have to have the access code for the keypad in order to get in."

"We knew that part. About the keypad."

"Yeah, but look." He pulls up a report and highlights a chunk of it.

"It says the room had been cleaned since the last murder."

"Yes, but read further."

62

I start reading out loud. "We interviewed the Dean of the University of Florida in Gainesville. We were told that the basement in the Science Building was not cleaned by the university." I look at Matt. "Holy shit."

"They didn't have it cleaned. Keep going."

I look back at the screen. "We interviewed the Head of the Science Department. We were told that they didn't have the basement cleaned, and that it wasn't their responsibility to do so. They directed us back to the Dean." I lean back. "So no one cleaned it."

"Nope. No one cleaned it. At least no one from the university."

"So who did then? It's obviously been cleaned. It's like it's a clean slate. Just start over."

"Whoever cleaned it has access to the basement. And they've changed that code after each murder. So it's someone they trusted the code with. The list has gotten smaller and smaller."

"Have they interviewed any of them? Eliminated them? How are we just getting this list now?"

"It was just sent over with the email. I think they were probably interviewing and wanted to finish them before they handed off the investigation."

I growl low. "We should have gotten that list as soon as they had it."

"I agree. But we didn't. Now we have it."

"So, are these the people that we can't find alibis for?"

"Yep. These are the ones who can't prove their whereabouts."

"We can't exactly question them. Who is on the list?"

Matt shows me the list as he gets up and stretches. "I need a drink." He heads for the fridge to grab a couple sodas.

"I don't recognize any of those names."

"Me either."

He sits back down next to me, handing me the soda. I go back to the crime scene photos. After what seems like hours, my eyes finally start to blur. I stand up and stretch. I walk around the dorm and do lunges down the narrow hall. Anything to stretch out my cramped up back.

I turn and do lunges back down the hall into our small living room. Matt is pouring over the crime scene photos. I look outside our tiny window and notice the sun is setting. I stare in shock for a moment.

"Fuck. The sun is going down. We've been at this for a good fifteen hours."

"Holy... shit..."

"Yeah. I know. That was my thought."

"No. No, not that. Come here."

I look at him curiously. "Okay." I walk over to him and sit. "What?"

He points to the crime scene photo on the table. "Recognize them?"

I look at the image for a moment. It's difficult to recognize anything about them, given how badly they look. One of them is almost unrecognizable. I look a little longer, squinting a little as I tilt my head. I pick up the photo.

My breath hitches when I see it. "Holy... shit..."

Matt looks at me. "Where was it we saw them? The rally? In a class? Because I know them. I know I know them."

"What are their names?"

"Alan Zurich. He's the one who was beaten. And Peter Miller. He's the one who was shot."

I think, trying to place the names. After a few moments, I shake my head. "I don't know. I can't think of it, but I know we've seen them."

"We'll have to see if anyone is missing in our classes this week."

"What's the report say on it?"

"It's not complete. But it's just like the rest. Anonymous call to 911 just after two in the morning. The commotion got the attention of passersby. A couple guys recognized them. Said they had just come from the Order of the Alpha Omega. They -"

"Wait. What?"

Matt looks over at me confused. "They just came from the Order of the Alpha Omega. Frat party. They recognized them. Identified them."

"Stop." I dive into the written reports in front of me. My eyes scan each report. "Fuck. I knew it. Look." I start laying down reports. "Order of the Alpha Omega." I lay down another. "Order of the Alpha Omega." I lay down another and point. "Order of the Alpha Omega. They all went to a party thrown by the Order of the Alpha Omega. All of them. The night before they were murdered."

"They could've been picked from the party and the murder went on from when they were picked to when it was called in. Look." Matt pulls the Medical Examiner's report. "M.E. puts the murder between midnight and two in the morning." He pulls the reports I had just laid down. "All of these reports have each victim at the Order of the Alpha Omega. That they had just come from the party. Just saw them at a party. This one says they were seen less than two hours before they were found. How the fuck was something like this kept from us?"

I scrub my hands down my face. "Can we really trust drunk frat guys?"

"Can we afford not to?"

I rub my eyes. "So what do we do with all of this? It's late. No way Brody is in."

"Call him at home. If we're working all day and night, so is he."

I call Brody and explain everything we've come up with. By the time I hang up I'm suddenly far too exhausted to think. "Now what?"

"Now. We go to bed. The Order of the Alpha Omega has an all day charity event tomorrow."

I smile and chuckle as I shake my head. "And let me guess. We're going?"

"Yes. We're going. Which means we have another long day ahead of us."

I groan. "They have some kind of a party tomorrow night."

He nods. "We're going to that, too." He stands and offers me a hand. I take it, and he pulls me up. "But first we need sleep. I don't think you're going to last another second."

I chuckle. "Always the one taking care of everyone else."

"Fucking right."

Matt leads me to the bedroom. I yawn a few times as I undress. I have no idea if I've managed to get more than my shirt off, though, before I'm crawling into bed. Seconds after my head hits Matt's arm, I'm asleep.

65

Chapter Eight

★ Matt ★

I open my eyes to the harsh Florida sunlight with a groan. I've been meaning to get blackout curtains so we're not constantly woken up at the crack of dawn when the sun starts to rise over the horizon. I love Florida. I love long days with plenty of sunlight. What I do not love in the slightest way is being woken up by it before five in the morning. Especially when I've had a long night and would like nothing more than to sleep in.

Apparently, though. That isn't in the cards. I reach over as my phone rings and pick it up. "What?" I growl, not bothering to look at the caller ID.

"The thing you two saw. It's a nametag," Brody says.

I sit bolt upright forgetting completely that DJ is laying on my chest. He startles and looks up at me. My heart beats faster. Excitedly. "A nametag? From where? What's the name?"

"Don't get too excited. We can't read the name. We can see an E and S. Lab is working on it. Name is too faded. No one can make anything out. But the lab has ways of figuring shit like this out."

"How long?" I ask impatiently.

"I don't rush the work of a genius. I learned my lesson well with you and DJ. But they said a couple of days. At least. Meanwhile I got the schedule for Order of the Alpha Omega DJ sent. I want you both at this week's events. All of them."

"Already planned on it. They have a huge event for charity today, and a celebration party tonight. DJ and I already planned on going. They have a carnival planned and everything for the kids in the community."

"Listen. Observe. Talk to people. Get me fucking anything." Brody hangs up.

I toss my phone back on the nightstand and look down at DJ. I look him up and down, realizing for the first time since I woke up that he's lying on his back in all his glory watching me. He has his hands interlocked behind his head. A soft smile plays at the corner of his mouth. His dark, jade eyes sparkle.

His perfectly sculpted chest and chiseled abs call to me. I wouldn't be able to stop myself from turning to him and reaching out to touch him if I tried. I lay down next to him and splay my hand over his chest and slowly slide it down over his stomach.

"What was that about?" he asks as he watches me.

"The thing under the broiler. It was a nametag. But we didn't get lucky enough to get a name or where it came from. There was an E and S. They sent it to the lab to get the rest of the company name. The person's name was illegible."

"We don't know if that belonged to one of the two people he killed or him."

"No. But we know who the people were. So if the name doesn't match them…" I trail my fingertips down lower until I'm just at the base of his already swollen and hard dick.

"Then we at least have something to go on. Something to add to the list of evidence." He inhales sharply when I trail my fingertip from his balls up his length.

"One more thing to nail this fucker to the wall." I grab his dick in my hand and start stroking tantalizingly slowly.

"Mmm…" He arches into me and thrusts into my hand. "I don't mind waking up like this every morning for the rest of my life."

I lean in to kiss him as he closes his eyes. He reaches up and tangles his fingers in my hair, pulling me to him and deepening the kiss.

We both moan. I start twisting my wrist and stroking more firmly, though not increasing my pace in the slightest. He arches and moans as his tongue flicks across mine. I nip his and suck lightly.

He moans and growls low as he pulls back. He pushes me onto my back and kisses me hard and deeply again and again. He starts stroking my dick at the same slow, firm pace I'm using on him. I arch into him again and again as he thrusts into my hand. It's his turn to nip my tongue and suck lightly on it. It draws a growl from deep within as we both get harder and harder for each other.

DJ pulls back and shifts so his back is to me. My eyes widen as I watch him straddle me. He lowers his mouth to my dick and licks my tip. I take his in my hand and wrap my other arm around his hips, bringing him to my mouth. I lick his tip and nip at his dimple. He sucks hard on my tip, making my dick jerk.

"Oh God," I say against his cock before taking more and more of him in my mouth until he's buried in my throat. I grip his hips and push him up before pulling him back down. I suck hard and graze his tip with my teeth after scraping lightly along his length.

"Matt…" He starts bobbing his head up and down over my dick, licking and sucking hard before nipping my length. I thrust into his mouth.

We both hum low and growl against each other as we suck and swallow around each other's tips. I suck up and down his vein hard before burying him in my throat and nipping him. I swallow around him moaning.

He sucks hard on my tip before moving lower and lower to suck on my balls. He nips along my length before sucking once more hard on my tip. He buries me in his throat and mimicks me. He swallows with a low moan.

My dick jerks and throbs for him just as his does for me. He thrusts into my mouth as fast as he's begun bobbing his head over my dick. We both scrape our teeth lightly over each other's length with each thrust.

"Fuck! DJ, I'm gonna come!" My fingertips dig into his hips.

"Oh God, me too."

We both bury ourselves in each other's mouths and suck hard, swallowing around each other's dicks. I come hard. My come shoots down his throat as my hips jerk in rhythm to each spurt of come. He pulls back slightly and swallows everything I give him.

As I come, DJ comes at the same time. He thickens and throbs in my mouth. The warm, salty, tangy liquid shoots down my throat. I greedily swallow it like it's the greatest thing I have ever tasted. And it just might be.

After we both stop coming and trembling, we lick each other clean. DJ pulls away and shifts once more. He collapses on the bed next to me as we both pant. I run my fingers through his hair as he traces the muscles of my chest and stomach. We catch our breath and come down.

"Why does it feel so much better coming down your throat than anyone I've ever been with?" I ask. I turn and kiss his head.

"Because you love the fuck out of me."

I laugh. "It's insane. But I do. I do love you. And after all these years it feels good to finally be able to say it."

"Not having to hide?"

"I don't want to hide." I shake my head. "Maybe being with you and being able to express my feelings for you is what changed my mind in not wanting to come out. But I'm not afraid anymore. I know how I feel. I don't care that it's only been a couple weeks."

"I'm not sure I really understand it myself, but I don't care either. I don't want to hide it anymore. Maybe I've just decided I'm too old for that shit. Or maybe it's because I'm finally able to tell you how I feel. And show it. And it feels pretty damn good. I don't want to lose that."

I smile and look down at him. "So? Where do we go from here? Do we have some big coming out party?"

"Why the hell do we need to announce to the world that we're together? We're two people who fell in love. Does anything else really matter?"

"Always had a way with words."

He looks up at me. "I'm sorry."

I raise an eyebrow. "For what?"

"Not telling you the way I felt a long time ago. I should've been brave. I should've just told you how I feel."

"It's not all on you, baby. I should've told you, too. Besides, we've apologized numerous times for this. It's done. Over."

"It doesn't matter. We know now. And we can move forward."

"Speaking of moving forward... we need to get up and get to the carnival."

DJ groans. "The only good about this is the kids."

I smile. "I'll admit it's fun to watch them have fun."

"You can say it. You don't like kids."

"I like some kids. My nieces and nephew. Layne." I pretend to think really hard. "Yeah. That's it."

DJ laughs as he starts getting up. "It's probably time to get ready to go. Otherwise... well, we aren't leaving this bed."

I laugh and get up with him. After we get cleaned up and dressed, we head for University Square, where the Order of the Alpha Omega has set up this charity event. We pay our entrance fee, and I can't help but notice which charity is benefiting from this year's carnival.

I elbow DJ. "Boys and Girls Club."

He eyes me confused. "So?"

I smile and chuckle. I lead him closer to the banner announcing the charity. "It wouldn't be a big deal. Except... this." I point to the Gainesville Police logo at the bottom as DJ reads what it says out loud.

"Proudly working with Gainesville Police to bridge the gap between our youth and our police officers by bringing them together with this carnival and donating all proceeds to the Club." He blinks. "What the fuck did I just read? I didn't know GPD was working with the Order of the Alpha Omega. Wouldn't that have been something we'd been made aware of?"

"DJ. Look around. Do you see any cops here?" I scan the crowd with him. "There's no one here I recognize from the department."

"They're fucking calling us out."

"That's what I think, too. Let's walk around. See what kind of information we can find."

DJ and I walk hand in hand through the carnival. We stop at booth after booth until we're both so hungry we're about to collapse. Thank God there's numerous food trucks and food booths around. After getting a giant corndog, the two of us start walking around more.

"So... is it just me, or does no one have any idea what we're talking about?" DJ asks, biting into his corndog.

"No. You aren't the only one." I stop at a balloon popping booth. I stand off to the side and watch as a very cute, young little girl throws a dart with all her might at a balloon. She squeals when it pops. I smile. The kid

70

behind the booth gives her a small purple teddy bear as her prize. She hugs it close as she skips away with her mother.

"Well, that was adorable," DJ says next to me.

"I got lucky with this booth. I've gotten a lot of little kids. They're beyond excited when they pop a balloon, but they jump up and down when I hand them their prize," the kid says to us as he turns. His smile falters when he notices how close the two of us are standing, but to his credit, he chokes it back and ignores it.

I've been pretty surprised at the lack of insults hurled our way. This fraternity's name says everything we need to know about it. And their mission statement confirms it. The club is very staunchly against same-sex relationships.

"I bet it feels pretty good to be donating the proceeds to the Boys and Girls Club," I say.

"Oh, for sure, man. We try to pick different charities every single year and host a huge event."

"That's awesome," DJ says. "I saw you're working with GPD, too. I heard they do a lot with the Boys and Girls Club."

The kid looks at us both completely bewildered. "I have no idea what you're talking about. We support the police department, but this is put on one hundred percent by us. Expensive as fuck, too."

"Oh," I say, portraying a little confusion myself. "Your banner at the entrance. It says that you're doing this with GPD."

"That's impossible. Man, are you serious? I'm the President of this chapter of Order of the Alpha Omega. I had that sign made special for this event. I assigned it to one of my brothers myself."

"Oh. Shit, we didn't know. We just saw it. Thought it was cool. We love what you're doing," I say.

"No. It's okay. Thanks for bringing it to my attention." He glares towards the entrance. "Hey, can you watch this booth? Pretty easy to run. Take the money. They hit a balloon, they get a small bear. They hit two balloons, they get what they want. Three darts. If they hit nothing, I give them a mini beanie. I need to take care of this."

DJ and I glance at each other before he jumps behind the booth. "Yeah. Fuck. You need to deal with it."

The kid jumps over the small counter in front of him and jogs towards the entrance. I look back at DJ. "That was interesting."

"Definitely interesting. I think we found our talker."

I look down as a little blonde haired girl tugs on my jeans. "May I help you, miss?" I ask her, throwing on my best southern charm as I kneel in front of her.

"I like balloons." Her blue eyes light up with her smile.

"Me, too." I smile brightly for her, and she beams.

"Can I play balloons?"

"Oh... I don't know," I say mock seriously. "Are you a big girl?"

Her eyes brighten even more. "Big girl!"

I smile. "How old are you?"

She holds out four fingers. "I this many!"

"You're in luck! You have to be exactly this many." I hold out four fingers.

Her eyes widen. "I that many!"

"Then let me direct you to this fine gentleman." I hold my hand out towards DJ. He's smiling behind the booth.

"Can I play balloons?" she asks DJ as I stand.

"How many are you?" DJ asks suspiciously as he smiles. The little girl holds out four fingers. "You're the perfect age!" He kneels down and hands her the darts. "Okay. Take this dart. Hold it right here just like this."

I smile as I stand and step back slightly next to the man with her. I watch as DJ explains how to throw the dart. She pouts sadly when she misses but tries again. There's no one around the booth so he lets her throw dart after dart.

"Thank you for this," the guy says. "Her parents were killed in a wreck a few days ago. This is the first time she's smiled genuinely. My niece is an incredible little girl."

"I'm sorry to hear she lost her parents. How are you holding up?"

He looks at me surprised. "I don't think anyone has actually asked me that. Which really is okay. My focus has been her. But me? It's hard. I never wanted kids. My brother said if anything happened, though, I was the only one he trusted to take his girl. So we signed papers just after she was born. Never thought I'd see this day."

I pat his shoulder. "You must be doing something right. She's a great kid. She's happy. At least right now. That's all you can do."

He smiles as we watch his niece. "Thank you. That means a lot to me."

"Yay!" the little girl screams as a balloon pops. She jumps up and down and squeals. "I got it! I got it!" She claps her hands excitedly.

DJ high fives her. "Pick anything you want."

Her eyes widen as she mulls over her choices. Finally, she points to the giant unicorn. "That one!"

DJ stands and reaches up for the unicorn. "There you go. A magical unicorn for a princess." He hands her the unicorn, which is bigger than her, with a giant smile. She takes it enthusiastically as the president of the Order comes back.

Her uncle looks up at me as he takes the unicorn she handed him. "Thank you."

"Anytime."

DJ looks at the president as the little girl and her uncle walk away. "I owe you for that. She used about twenty darts before she hit one balloon, and I let her pick whatever she wanted." He reaches in his wallet and takes out a hundred dollar bill. He puts it in the till.

"Oh, holy shit. That's way too much. I'd have done the same," the president says.

"No big deal. It's for charity, right?"

"Yeah." He smiles as he climbs back behind the booth as DJ climbs out. "Thanks for taking care of the booth for me. The little fucker I assigned to the sign took off. Oliver might get knocked out this time. Too many bullshit antics. I might kick him out of the Order. I don't need that shit."

DJ and I glance at each other before looking back at him. I clear my throat. "This Oliver a troublemaker?"

"Oh, fuck yes. Wouldn't know it looking at him. But the more you get to know him, the more fucked up he gets." His attention falls on a kid running to his booth. He smiles.

"We better let you go," DJ says.

"Hey, thanks for keeping me company and taking care of the booth. We're having a party tonight. You both should come to the house." He pulls out a card and hands it to us. "You can watch me kick Oliver out of the Order. I'm done with his antics. This was the last straw. Small thing. But on top of so many?" He shakes his head as he turns to the little boy.

"Yeah, we'll see you there," I say, glancing at the card. It's all black with nothing more than a name and an address. On the back is

73

nothing more than a gold embossed number two. "Andrew Kennsington. That's you?"

"That's me. You two need that to get in. Don't lose it."

We nod as I tuck the card away. We hit a food truck on the way out and start walking back to our dorm.

I look at DJ. "I guess this is our in."

"I didn't know it was exclusive."

"Guess that means we need to work to get into the rest of them."

"Oliver. What do you make of him?"

"Not a clue. But we need to find out more. If he was the one who was in charge of that banner, why would he put that they are partnered with GPD when they aren't? It makes no fucking sense."

"We need to relay the information and look into it as best we can. All we can do for now."

DJ takes my hand as we near the dorm. I give it a light squeeze. Instincts have never steered me wrong before. I'll be damned if I don't trust them now.

Oliver.

There seems to be something more going on. And my gut says that it all somehow leads back to him.

Chapter Nine

☆ DJ ☆

Later that night, Matt and I arrive at the address on the card we got from Andrew. There's one person standing at the door. He's overly muscular and looks like a bouncer from a bar that's used to seeing a lot of trouble.

"Help you?" he growls as he looks us up and down. Matt and I are both tall, but this guy has to be close to seven feet.

"Uh. Yeah." I hand him the card. He looks at it a moment before flipping it around. He uses a small hole puncher and punches the head of a wolf into the bottom corner of the card and hands it back to me. I look at him bewildered.

He shakes his head. "That's a VIP card. Gives you access to all of our house events and parties. When it gets full, security or Mr. Kennsington will get you a new one. Show that card at the bar. You'll get the good stuff."

"The good stuff?" Matt asks curiously.

"Yeah. The good stuff. We have boxed wine. We have cheap beer. For VIP's you get the good wine from the Order's cellar. And the beer on tap. Trust me. That's the shit you want. The other stuff is from a watered

75

down keg. It's how they are able to provide such a large amount of alcohol."

I nod. "Okay. That's good to know."

The guard steps aside and lets us in. Matt turns to me after we enter. "Did that seem odd?"

"So fucking odd."

"Do we trust the bar?"

"Not a chance in hell."

We walk into the house further, following the loud as hell music. There are tons of people all over the place, but what throws me off is how many of them are guys kissing in corners. Or unabashedly in the open on the couch.

I pull Matt into a hall and lower my voice. "What the fuck is going on? Did I completely miss the look Andrew Kennsington gave us when he saw us standing close earlier?"

"No. I saw it, too. You didn't miss it."

I step into Matt when two girls run down the hallway in their bra and underwear holding hands and giggling. "Is this a fucking orgy?" I watch them in disbelief.

Matt reaches down for my hand. "Let's just walk around. See what we can find out. Observation. Greatest ally."

I follow as Matt starts walking through the house slowly to the backyard. The music is louder out here, and there's far more people. Several in the pool. We spot Andrew and beeline for him, becoming far more uncomfortable and confused as the seconds go on.

"Hey! There you guys are. Glad you could make it!" Andrew says as a guy next to him kisses him very deeply before walking away. I feel my mouth drop open, but I can't do anything about it. Andrew laughs. "Order of the Alpha Omega is a fraternity for gay men on campus. But we specifically chose the name we did so that we could keep our brothers safe. We even made up the mission statement so that people are thrown off. I'm sure you both are aware that many aren't accepting of us, and there's a serial killer on the loose. Our Founders wanted to make sure we were safe going forward. We're a pretty new fraternity. Only about fifteen years. I took over for my older brother."

"But... you..." I sputter, unable to spit the words running through my brain out of my mouth. I look at Matt for help.

He squeezes my hand with a chuckle. "You threw us with the look at the carnival."

"Test. Needed to see how you react."

I shake my head. "So this… it's a fraternity for gay men at the college?"

"It's a safe place. Yes." Something dark crosses his eyes before he looks down. "At least it has been. Until recently." He looks back up at us and signals us to a quiet part of the house. We sit down on some patio chairs in the corner of the backyard. He looks up at us. "Look. I overheard a conversation I wasn't supposed to when I was at the Dean's turning in our budget for the year. I know you both are cops. I verified it earlier. It's why I was gone for so long."

I shift uncomfortably and look at Matt. "What?"

"Your secret is safe. I haven't said a word. I won't. But I need your help. The murders of gay men on campus. They are members of the Order. All of them."

Matt glances at me then back at Andrew. "Tell us what you know."

"I don't know a lot. All I know is they are couples. Couples who have been members for a couple of years. They're all seniors. They were all good guys. Kept to themselves. These last two were truly some of the greatest. I considered them friends. We were hanging out at the last party we had. Alan went to the bathroom. He was gone for a while. Peter went to check on him. Neither came back."

"Did you look for them?" I ask.

Andrew nods. "I thought they went home. I called both of them. Sent them a text. I found out when the police contacted me that they had been the next victims. I'm positive I'm the top suspect at this point. I had nothing to do with any of it."

I shake my head. "You were eliminated as a suspect. We have a short list."

Andrew takes a shaky breath and swipes the backs of his hands over his eyes. "I'll do whatever I need to do to catch this guy. I feel like he's more targeting the Order then he is gay men."

"Do you have anyone you had some kind of a rift with lately? Did the Order have some kind of a falling out with anyone? What about that Oliver kid?" Matt asks.

"None that I've been able to think of. We're a pretty well-functioning organization. Oliver hasn't shown up tonight."

"Well, if you think of anything at all, come to us." I take out my wallet and look around before taking out a card. "Do you have a pen anywhere?" I watch as Andrew reaches in his pocket and pulls one out. I write both mine and Matt's personal numbers on the card. "Call us."

"And you're right," Matt says quietly. "We are undercover. We're here to help, but you need to help us."

"Anything you need," Andrew agrees. "And I want you to know. You're honorary members of the Order. That's a lifelong thing."

I nod with a small smile. "We understand the implications. It means a lot. Thank you."

"Just... please... Help me protect my brothers. You have free reign. We have nothing to hide. Explore. Ask questions. Just help us."

Matt puts his hand on Andrew's knee. "You can trust us. We'll figure it out. They didn't put us in here because we look pretty. They put us in here because we're the best in the department at what we do. We'll help. I promise."

He nods. "I don't even care if you guys are gay or not. Just help us."

I smile. "We are. Though our relationship didn't start, we didn't admit it, until the rally held on campus after we were first put undercover."

"That makes me feel a lot better. Crazy as that sounds. I guess it's comforting knowing we have a couple helping us instead of just a random investigator. Not that I don't believe they can do it, but I feel better having some people like us on our side."

I stand slowly. Matt follows. I look down at Andrew as he stands. "The whole department is behind you, Andrew. We'll figure it out."

Matt and I mingle for a little while longer. Most people keep bringing up the name Oliver. I decide we need to figure out who he is, but no one has seen him tonight.

Considering how fucked up he seems to be, he's one of my top suspects. Prone to fits of anger. Aggression. The very next second he's everyone's best friend. Making a huge dinner for the house. Quiet the second after that. Like he's so lost in his own mind that he can't hear anyone around him talking.

78

After a while, Matt and I check in with Andrew and say our goodbyes. We head back to our dorm. Neither of us say a word until we're back inside our room. I lock the door behind us. Matt goes directly to his laptop.

I watch him but say nothing. I know better than to say a word when he's mulling things over in his head. It's best to just give him something to drink and make sure he takes a sip or two every now and then.

I look at my watch after a couple of hours and decide that considering we still have to act like college students and attend classes, we need to go to sleep. "Matt."

"Hmm...?" he grumbles, not looking up at me.

"Matt. It's time for bed."

"Not yet. I need to finish this."

"No." I stand and grab his laptop. I close everything out and shut down as he watches me incredulously. "It's one in the morning. We have a class at ten."

"You realize I'm a grown ass man."

"Then act like it. We can come back to this tomorrow. We still have a job to do."

"I was doing my job." He gestures to the laptop.

"You know what I mean. Enough for the night. Bed." I put the laptop down and stand over him with my arms crossed. His dark brown eyes flash in anger, but I don't flinch.

Finally, he stands. "Fine. You're right. Things were starting to look a little blurry."

"I could tell. By the amount of times you rubbed your eyes. Now. Please. Bed."

He smiles as he chuckles and shakes his head. He turns for the bedroom, taking my hand and pulling me with him. "I just got Alphaed by the Beta."

I laugh. "Beta's job is to take care of Alpha when Alpha is too busy to realize he needs to pay attention to himself." I slap his ass. "But you can fuck right off if you think you're the Alpha.

He laughs and squeezes my hand. "Is that true?"

"Of course it's fucking true. Did you forget the giant painting in my den of a wolf pack?"

79

He shakes his head. "No. I didn't. I like that painting." Matt closes the door.

Before I have time to react, I'm backed against the door. Matt is pressed against me and his mouth and hands are all over me. I can't think about anything but his tongue down my throat. He lifts off my shirt, making me instantaneously miss his warmth. He tosses his wherever mine ended up, and his mouth is once more, blessedly, on mine.

I groan. "Holy shit. What are you doing?" I dig my fingertips into his shoulders as he nips at my Adam's apple. "Oh fuck."

"I'm not tired." He trails his tongue to the side of my neck. He squeezes my dick as he gently bites my shoulder.

"Oh God!" I gasp out a breath and grip him as he somehow undoes the button of my jeans without me feeling it.

He takes my dick in his hands and pumps hard. I moan gutturally and damn near slide down the door. If his rock solid body wasn't firmly against mine, I probably would be on the floor. I fumble to keep a grip on anything I can as he brings me closer and closer to edge with each pump, stroke, and flick against my tip.

Just as I'm about to come, though, Matt starts tugging me to the bed. He finishes taking off both of our clothes on the way, though it's only a few steps. He crawls into the bed, not taking his hand off my dick. I have no choice but to follow.

Matt sits on his knees. I shuffle to him, a little confused at the devilish look he has in his eyes. I don't have a single second to question him. His lips once again crash to mine. He squeezes my dick lightly, but doesn't stroke or move it.

After a long, very deep kiss, Matt slowly releases his grip. He moves back a little as he lets go. He nods towards the bed. My eyes widen in unabashed want and hungry need when I realize what he wants. I eagerly drop, gripping the pillows and watching him over my shoulder.

Matt gently rubs my ass before he runs one finger over it. I close my eyes and moan when he starts teasing my ass with his tip. My eyes roll back in my head when I feel his thick tip start to enter me. I damn near come when he pulls it out and puts it back in. Slowly. Torturously slowly.

"Oh… fuck…," I moan into the pillows.

"God, I didn't know it would feel this good," Matt whispers as he groans in ecstasy.

I relax more and more the further and deeper his silk-encased, hard as steel cock sinks into me. He pulls it all the way out and pushes a little deeper into me with each thrust. I'm so high off him and the feeling of him, I'm sure I'll never be able to come down.

His thick cock stretches me in ways I only dreamed. The feeling of him thrusting into me is better than anything I've ever imagined. I push back into him with each slow, firm thrust, until he's so deep inside me that I don't know where I even begin.

My ass clenches around him as he throbs inside me. He continues to pull all the way out and thrust all the way back in. Faster. Deeper. Harder. I pant and moan and writhe as I push back against him with each and every thrust. I reach down and start tugging on my dick as I moan.

"Oh fuck, don't stop," I whisper breathlessly. "Don't fucking stop."

He reaches down, swatting my hand away and starts jerking my dick at the same pace he's slamming into me. His balls slap my ass with every jerk of his hips. He strokes my dick firmly and hard until the sensation of him pounding my ass and stroking my dick is too much for me to take. My dick starts throbbing and pulsing.

"Come, baby. Come for me," he rumbles in my ear.

I want to tell him I'm about to come all over the fucking sheets, but as soon as I feel his dick start jerking inside me as his come fills my ass, I come so hard, I see stars. Bright, blinding stars exploding in front of my eyes.

"Oh fuck! Matt! Holy fuck!" I can feel my come gushing out of me soaking the sheets, his hand, and my thighs, but I don't care. His hot come filling my ass as he slows his thrusts and thrusts both of us through the trembling orgasm is all I care about.

"Oh God, DJ! Oh fuck! Yes!"

His strokes on my dick slow as I writhe and moan. We pant and tremble. We don't move for a few moments until our breathing slows.

After several long minutes, Matt slowly starts to pull out of me. He releases his grip on my dick and grasps my hips. I can feel him pulling his come as he pulls out. Before long, it's dripping down my ass. Matt shifts and slowly falls on his back next to me.

I look at him and literally curl into his side. I've never been one for the afterglow of sex. I've always preferred that it end quickly, and the

81

person next to me just leaves. But not with Matt. With Matt, I want it all. I want the whole damn universe.

"We should probably clean up," I say against his chest.

He groans and pulls me up with him. "Probably."

A few minutes later, the two of us are lying comfortably in bed on fresh sheets. Matt holds me tight and close. I lock an arm around his waist and lean up to kiss him. His tongue twines with mine. He easily dominates the kiss. I let him without hesitation, though I've never been the one to let anyone have control.

Just him.

He's the only one I've ever felt comfortable enough with to give it to.

He pulls back and runs his thumb over my lower lip. "I was putting down everything we learned today."

I shake my head. "Don't. I don't want to talk about the case tonight. I just want you."

I push him on to his back. I lean down and kiss him as his hands trail featherlight up my thighs to my ass. He slides back into me with a low moan and thrusts slow and deep as I arch for him.

For the first time in my life, I let someone make love to me. And when he's done, I make love to him. Over and over again until we're both so exhausted we can't move.

We fall into a deep sleep wrapped in each other's arms as the sun starts coming up.

Satisfied.

Happy.

Content.

Chapter Ten

☆ Matt ☆

DJ and I sit near the back of the theater and watch the chaos unfold in front of us. I never really knew how much work went into a theater production. Lights. Lines. Costumes. Music. Everything running in perfect harmony.

"How many times must I tell you, Selena," the director begins. "Say your lines with emotion! You're not a robot!"

I chuckle as I watch. "Tell me again why they're making us take this class?"

"Because of Lang. Investigation pointed him out as one suspicious motherfucker."

"Well, at least he's been ruled out."

"Where is he anyway?"

I point to the tall, very lanky, emo looking guy at the side of the stage. "Glaring at the director."

"I don't know what this guy's deal is. I think he's yelled at everyone from lighting to the lead actress."

"Dude has a stick up his ass." I watch as Lang shakes his head and walks to the back of the darkened theater to where we are.

He sits next to me. "I joined theater to actually hone my skills. Not to sit out and watch everyone else fuck up. Fuck, I hate that guy."

I chuckle. "Tell me again why he didn't pick you for the lead? I've seen you act."

"Because I'm too good. But his excuse? Don't have the right look. Like I can't lose the black eyeliner and nail polish." He holds his hand out and wiggles his fingers. "I'd even lose the lip piercing. Nose piercing is small enough to not be noticed on stage. I don't think they'd notice the eyebrow ring, but fuck. I'd lose that, too."

"He's just afraid of you," DJ says. "Too intimidating for him."

"Too different from him. I don't wear slacks and polo shirts and fit in his stupid little clique."

"I still don't understand how that little prick ended up the director of this show," I say.

"He's probably fucking the professor. He seems to like sucking up to her. And they do disappear a lot," Lang says.

DJ covers his mouth to stifle his laugh. "I shouldn't laugh."

"Why not? It's funny. Chick is like eighty years old," Lang says. "Probably feels like fucking dust."

I slap my hand over my mouth, but it's too late. The laugh was loud and echoed through the theater. Director Dick looks towards the back. "Oh, here we go," I mumble.

"Something funny back there, Rejects?"

I raise an eyebrow and keep my voice low. "Rejects?"

"He really did just say that," DJ says, astonished.

"Nothing funny back here. Just watching a pencil dick direct a show above his talent," Lang says loud enough for him to hear.

"Damn, I like you more and more," I say a little in awe of his ability to not give a shit.

"That's it! Out!" Director Dick says.

"Why don't you come back here and make me," Lang growls. Director Dick huffs and puffs but says nothing. "He'll tattle to his girlfriend. I'll get reprimanded. Happens every week. I don't really care."

"I think this guy is a little power hungry," DJ says quietly.

"Reminds me of another little prick I know. Dude in my frat house. Name is Oliver."

I look at DJ before looking back at Lang. "First of all, you're part of a frat?"

Lang nods. "Order of the Alpha Omega. I saw you guys at the party the other day. Talking to the Prez. Overheard a little bit, but don't worry. Secret's safe with me. I already knew."

I shake my head. "Are we that obvious?"

"Oh. No, it's nothing like that. I was with Andrew in the Dean's office when you both were talking about coming in undercover. I didn't say anything because it wasn't my place. I didn't really care anyway. And I ended up liking you both."

I scrub my hands down my face. "I can't believe you're in a frat. Nothing wrong with it. I just can't believe it. Especially that one. My gaydar must be off." I smile at him with a chuckle. "Good for you, though. I'm happy I'm getting to know the real person behind..." I gesture over him. "All of that."

He laughs quietly. "Trust me. I hadn't intended on it. But a couple years ago, I met the man I fell in love with. Last year, we were recruited by the Order and were accepted. Probably the best decision I ever made to accept the recruitment because I got kicked out of the dorms. Couldn't pay for the room and board. After I came out, my parents cut me off. Only way I'm able to afford tuition is working on campus. And I have a part time job I work. But I live at the house. If they hadn't accepted us, I'd be living in a refrigerator box."

"Good thing you got in," DJ says.

"My boyfriend would have taken me in, but I'm not there yet, you know?"

"Understandable," I say. "Takes time. Take things at the pace that feels comfortable. That's always the best thing to do."

He smiles. "I still can't believe I opened up to you the way I have. I never do that."

DJ grins. "He's easy to talk to."

"I'm also as much of an asshole as you are," I tease.

"Fuck. You're probably more of an asshole."

I smile and put my feet up on the chair in front of me. "What about this Oliver? I've heard a lot of shit about that guy."

"Seems like a real piece of work," DJ says.

"Oh, he is. And then some. He was already in the Order when we rushed. I'm pretty sure he's been there since damn near when Andrew became President. And that was three years ago when he was a sophomore. He took over for his older brother. Honestly, I think Oliver resents that."

"Why would he resent that?" I ask.

"Well, he was just a freshman then. But I've heard him bitching about how Andrew gets handed everything because of his family. The Kennsington's are really a well-to-do family. But they are also the founders of the club. It was founded by Andrew's uncle."

"Yeah?" DJ asks, a little surprised.

"It's pretty rare to see that many gay men in one family. But it happened. Their uncle founded it. He handed it down to one of his friends who embodied all of the core values and helped him found it. It was then handed down to another member who was definitely someone to live up to. When Andrew's brother took over, there were only about thirty members. At the end of his reign, there were fifty. Now we have almost a hundred. He's a good leader. But, most importantly, he's a good guy. Non-judgemental. A genuine person." He looks over at us. "It's why I don't hate him."

I smile. "I get it."

"Oliver, though. He's always been off to me. I've never liked him. One second he's your best friend. The next he's your worst enemy. He lurks. You won't even know the guy is around. He listens quietly to conversations that don't involve him. Brings them up later like he was there and part of it. He weasels his way into gatherings between just a few people having a private conversation. But mostly, I've always thought he was a little obsessed with Andrew."

"Obsessed?" DJ asks. "How? More than just a jealousy fueled obsession?"

"Oh, fuck yes. He's always around Andrew. And if he isn't, he's watching him. I've brought it up a couple of times. Andrew doesn't really seem to think he's any harm, so I've let it go. But the last party? Andrew was dancing with his boyfriend after you both left. They went upstairs to Andrew's room. And I thought Oliver was going to spontaneously combust. Shit. He was pissed. Started throwing and slamming things around before he finally left. We didn't even know he was there. No one saw him the entire party. He just fucking appeared."

I glance at DJ. "Sounds like he wants him for himself."

DJ shrugs. "I don't know. I get a totally different type of vibe from that."

I raise an eyebrow. "Like…?"

DJ leans forward, resting his hands on the seat in front of him. He turns and looks back at us. "What if it's not about jealousy? What if it's about what you and I feared about coming out in the first place? Hatred."

I furrow my brows and cross my arms over my chest. "But he's gay. Isn't that kind of a prerequisite to being part of the Order?"

"Or he acts that way. To stalk his victims," Lang says. "I've never seen him with a guy or a girl."

"Well, would he be if he wants Andrew?" I ask.

"I would. I'd want him to notice me. Make him jealous," Lang counters.

"It's what we've done for I don't even know how long," DJ says quietly.

"That's true." I can't deny that we've both been idiots. I sigh and rub my head. "What other stuff?"

"Well. He's a science geek," Lang continues. "Always hanging around the science building. One day, I was walking to my science class and saw him near the back of the building. Looked like he was sneaking around, but I couldn't be sure. He's always doing science-y shit. For all I knew, he was taking a soil sample to see what kinds of birds crapped in the area." He shrugs. "But then a couple days later, the first murders took place. I don't know what to make of that. I haven't seen him in that area since."

I shift uncomfortably as small things start niggling at me. I look at my watch. "How the fuck is there still an hour left of this shit show?" I growl under my breath.

"It's your last class. That's a plus," Lang says.

I stare straight ahead, chewing on the inside of my cheek. There's so many little things that have been happening that have stuck with me. The nametag we still haven't heard about. This thing with Oliver and that banner at the charity event. It was a blatant call out for us. And if he's the one who had the sign done…

Then, there are the crazy mood swings. Pissed off one second. Cooking dinner for his brothers the next. Throwing what I can only call a

87

tantrum when he sees Andrew going off with his boyfriend. Being seen around the Science Building.

All of the people killed were a part of the Order. That had to have been known when DJ and I got put undercover. Why weren't we told? Why did that become such a surprise that was sprung on us? Why weren't we shown the initial list?

I shake my head. "Fuck. I need to get out of here." I turn to Lang. "Can you cover for us?"

"Sure thing. Sneak out the back corner door. He won't see you. I do it all the time. You'll be at the party Saturday?"

"Yeah. Yeah we'll be there." I stand and look down at Lang. "Thank you."

"Anytime."

I gently push DJ towards the exit Lang directed us to. When we get outside, I take a deep breath. The air is fucking hot and stifling, but it's fresh. I take another deep breath and shake my head again.

"I need to walk. I just need to fucking walk."

"Okay. Let's walk." DJ takes my hand. We walk aimlessly for several minutes before he says anything. "What happened in there? You got quiet as fuck."

"Same as the other night. There's so much running through my head. I just need to run through it and figure it out. Or at least get it out of my head."

"Talk to me. Run through it."

"The problem is I don't understand any of it. I don't understand how it fits in place with everything else."

He squeezes my hand. "Then run me through it."

"Why weren't we told about the full list? And the nametag. How was that missed? Why don't we have anything back from the lab yet?" I look at him as we walk. "Why weren't we told that every victim was a brother of the Order?"

He looks at me a moment before we both look in front of us again. "I don't know. Maybe that's something we need to ask the Chief and Brody."

I sigh and scrub my hand down my face keeping hold of his hand as we near a food truck on the food truck block near the University. We order a couple of burgers and sit down at a table in a surprisingly quiet area in the busy block.

"Then the restaurant. That kid. What happened to him? And why is there a nametag at a crime scene of two gay guys the very next day after he gets fired by fucking with two gay guys?"

"I'd say coincidence but…" He shrugs.

"I don't believe in coincidence. Neither do you." I take a bite and chew methodically. "And then there's this shit with Oliver. Why does his name keep coming up? And why did he specifically call out GPD?"

"There's something fucked up with him. I can't figure it out. He's suspicious."

"He's seen around the Science Building? He seems to have an obsession with Andrew."

"Or a hatred of gays."

"I'd like to talk to him. Maybe we need to start hanging around the Order."

"Might come off as suspicious if we just start showing up. The party is in a couple of days. Until then, maybe we need to focus on piecing together everything we do have with all of the other shit in the case files."

I know he's right. But the holes are pissing me off. This is the messiest case I've ever been given. I don't like it. I like order. I like neat. Even the most fucked up cases I've been given have had some kind of order to them. This case is so far over the line of chaos, I'm not entirely certain that anything I've been thinking is close to being on the right path.

"You know…" I look up at DJ. "This may be unconventional, but isn't Lang in the Forensic Science and Criminology program?"

DJ looks at me suspiciously. "What are you thinking?"

"Fresh eyes. What if he looked? Saw something we don't see."

DJ looks around and hisses, "Are you crazy? You can't just allow someone off the streets to look at this case."

I sigh and look at him. "I trust him. I can't explain it. But I think he might be able to see what we're missing. I've looked at those files over and over. You have, too. We're stuck. It's the same shit again and again. We're just getting thrown in this loop. Nothing fits. It's a jumbled fucking mess. And in situations like this, I usually bring the case to someone else to look at. I call you in. I have Mariah go over it. Or Lyric. Just… anything to get me out of the rut."

"Okay. Okay. I trust your instincts." He looks up at me. "You're right. We need to get out of this rut. I feel like there's just a bunch of information thrown at us that should fit somewhere, but doesn't. I don't like it."

"Me either." I stand and start gathering our garbage. I throw it away just as my phone rings. "Yeah," I bark into the receiver as DJ and I start walking.

"That nametag?" Brody asks into the receiver.

I look at my phone a second, a little surprised that I'm getting the call right after I was complaining about not having the results. "What about them?"

"Name on the tag is Oliver. Restaurant is Amelia's."

I blink and stop walking. "Holy shit. Are you sure?"

"Positive. What do you got?"

"I don't know. I'll call you back." I hang up the phone. DJ is looking at me. "Fucking Amelia's. Name on the tag? Oliver."

DJ's mouth falls open. "Are you joking? That's way too fucking easy, and it doesn't all make sense. No way he pulled that off on his own if he did at all. How the fuck did he get two guys down there with no one seeing?"

"I know, DJ. We need to get back and figure this out. I'll call Lang. He can meet us. I'd call Lyric and Mariah, but we need someone who can understand the things we aren't trained for."

"I don't want either of them anywhere near this case, Matt. Something is off. It's been bothering me. I don't like it."

We both walk a little faster as I call Lang. By the time we get back to the dorm, Lang is already there. We work long into the night. We all sleep late into the morning and skip classes as we work through the day. By the time night rolls around, we're all so tired we can't move.

But I was right about Lang. He did see a lot of things we didn't. Things that make everything make so much fucking sense. The only problem is I don't know what to do with the information. And I don't like any of it.

When DJ finally lays next to me on the floor in our bedroom, I give him a soft kiss and cuddle him close. Layne is curled up on the bed with Mariah and Lyric. We called them here because we don't at all like what we've found out. The three of them have all fallen into a deep peaceful sleep.

"This is going to get really bad, isn't it?" DJ mumbles into my chest.

"We have a plan. In the morning, Mariah and Lyric take Layne to Disney. That's how we keep them far away from this."

"They aren't happy we aren't telling them what's going on."

"They don't need to be happy. They need to be safe. Not having any information and being checked into the hotel under a false name is part of that. This will all be over tomorrow night. Then we can explain it."

"If we survive it," he says quietly. I can feel his tears against my chest. I push him back slightly and kiss him deeply before wiping away his tears. I pull him back into me. He wraps me in his arms just as tightly.

"We'll survive it, DJ. There isn't another option."

Chapter Eleven

☆ DJ ☆

"We stay together. That's the plan," Matt says as we walk through the frat house.

"Got it," I say.

Matt takes my hand as we walk and stop to talk to those who stop us. My mind races. Though I try to calm it, it's no use. It completely flies into another galaxy. The only thing keeping me on the ground and not chasing after it is Matt. My strength and bravery and courage when mine is totally gone.

I'm worried about my son. I'm worried about Lyric and Mariah. My family. Though, they've checked in and everything is fine. They all just went to sleep. Safe and sound in a comfy bed miles away from here.

We'd learned that Oliver was indeed the server at Amelia's the night DJ and I went out on our date. He was the one who had been fired for his blatant homophobic slurs. The couple who had been murdered that night was the young gay couple in the corner booth near us. Very quiet. Didn't say a word. Just enjoying each other's company.

Suddenly, things started coming together in ways they simply hadn't before. Every couple that had been murdered had been a couple that had been close to Andrew. A couple who seemingly blatantly ignored Oliver, or had gotten into some kind of a blowout argument with him. And they all had experienced a serious blow to the back of the head.

It was something neither me or Matt had seen. We both were so focused on the actual beating, we assumed the blow to the back of the head was just part of it. But Lang saw that the blow was the exact same on every single victim. And it looked like it came from the butt of a gun.

The interesting thing was the bullet that was found in the back of the head of the victims who had been shot didn't match the type of gun that the blow to the back of the head seemed to point to. Looking deeper, Lang found that the Medical Examiner had matched the blow to the butt of a Glock 19. Which is typically used by law enforcement.

The bullet itself came from Ruger LC9. Typically used as a backup weapon for most cops. I keep one on my ankle. Matt usually has one on his thigh. Though being undercover, he's kept his on his ankle.

It took us a little while to understand the entire thing of calling out GPD. It seemed pretty obvious to us that Oliver is seemingly working with someone either in law enforcement or retired or someone who has law enforcement experience. We figured out it wasn't him calling out GPD or taunting us. It was a clue.

The problem is we don't know what exactly it means. The more we looked, the more we realized that it has to be someone within our department. It's the only thing that would explain certain things. Like the suspect list not being given to us. Certain other information not being passed along to us.

And that… that is the reason we sent my son away with two of the only people I trust, other than Matt, to protect them. We don't know who the leak is, or how far up it goes. We haven't even told Brody or the Chief what's going on.

After what feels to me like hours talking to people, Matt leads me to the corner of the house and around the side. Away from everyone. It's quiet. No one is around, but we're still close enough to people that if anything happens, someone will hear it.

"Talk to me," Matt says quietly. He leans in and kisses me, relaxing me slightly. "Tell me what's going on."

"I'm fucking scared, Matt. I'm scared. There's unknowns."

93

"There's always unknowns. Even when we plan missions for SWAT down to the last damn detail. We can't account for everything. It's impossible. All we can do is be prepared to the best of our ability.

"We have no backup, Matt. We have no one that we can trust."

He takes my face in his hands. "We have Lang."

I look at him incredulously. "Lang. That's what we're going with?"

He smiles and turns back to the backyard. "Look around us. We have all of these guys for backup. We have Lang on Oliver. We have nearly a hundred guys watching our -" Matt starts falling forward. I turn and catch him quickly.

"What the fuck? Matt!" I catch movement out of the corner of my eye. Though I try to dodge it, I feel instant pain when something hard connects to the back of my head. Everything goes immediately dark.

★★★

I groan as I open my eyes. The pain that instantly shoots through me is intense enough to make me wish I'd never been born. The light is blurred. For a moment I feel like my stomach has relocated to my mouth. I unattractively dry heave as I try to remember what the fuck happened.

We were at the Order of the Alpha Omega's party. We were talking to almost everyone. We gathered a ton of information. I don't remember half of it. But it was a lot. Something about Oliver. Something I have to remember.

I cough and spit out blood as I turn over onto my stomach. I cough again against the cold, hard, cement floor and spit up more blood. I clench my hands into fists and bring my knees to my chest. I have to get up.

"Fuck," I groan. I shakily push myself to my knees. I blink a few times as I take several deep breaths. I'm in a basement. Cold. Dank. There are a few metal tables. Bunsen burners. "What the fuck?" I rub the back of my head and feel a sticky wetness. I bring my hand back around and see my fingertips covered with blood. My head snaps around when I hear a groan.

"Shit...," Matt moans. I hear metal against metal. As soon as I see him, my heart sinks. He's standing against a metal support beam with his

94

hands behind his back. Judging from the clang I hear as he moves, I know he's cuffed.

"No... Matt..." I start crawling towards him. I'm kicked hard in the ribs and fall back to the ground moaning and writhing in pain as I hold my sides and squeeze my eyes closed. I shake my head, forcing my eyes open.

I watch in total fear as a black SWAT boot comes down towards my head. I automatically put my hands up and shove as hard as I can, blocking the blow, as I scramble away. Keeping my hands in front of me, I wedge myself against a wall. I look up and my heart damn near stops beating.

"What? Can't figure out how the hell someone like me got you here?" Oliver spits at me. "Big guy like you can't be beaten by a guy like me?"

I keep one hand up and start reaching slowly for my ankle. "Look. I don't know what's going on here, but we have nothing to do with it." I feel along my ankle for my gun. Oliver reaches behind him.

"Looking for this?" He points my Ruger LC9 at me.

I put my other hand back up, my eyes trained on the gun for any opening I have to disarm him. "Shit," I whisper. My eyes flick to Matt when I hear him moan again. His head falls forward.

"Didn't think I was smart enough to find it? Cops. You're all so fucking stupid."

I swallow hard. "Cops?"

He rolls his eyes and throws my badge in its leather case at me. It bounces off my chest and lands on the ground in front of me. "Add the fact that you're gay on top of it, and you're just one big disappointment, aren't you?"

I shake my head trying to follow. Oliver shoots the gun. It pings off the wall a couple feet away from me. I do everything I can to stay calm as Matt moans again and whimpers. I don't have a chance to say a word, though, because the basement door opens. Matt groans and opens his eyes. He coughs and spits up blood just as I had as he opens his eyes. I take a second to thank whatever God is listening that he's okay.

"We talked about the noise, Oliver."

My eyes snap to the voice. I'd recognize it anywhere. "Brody."

"What the hell?" Matt groans confused.

95

"Sorry, dad."

"Shit...," I whisper. My eyes lock on Brody as he looks around.

"I didn't want you two involved in this. The problem is I got overruled. If the Chief would've left you out of it and let me assign the fuckers I wanted, you two would be just fine," Brody says almost sadly. He looks back at me. "The issue is that you two are too smart. As soon as the Chief picked you, I knew. I knew you'd be able to figure it out."

I shake my head, trying to follow. What the hell was it that we found out at the party that I needed to remember? "What the fuck are you talking about?" I ask.

"Ransoms," Matt moans. I can tell he's trying to fight to stay awake. All at once I remember.

I look up at Brody. "Ransoms. You ransomed the families. Of the other victims. That was never in any of the case files."

Brody smiles. "Pretty smart, huh? It was actually Oliver's idea."

Oliver grins proudly. "It was easy, really. The families happily stayed quiet because my dad is a cop. High-ranking officer. Trustworthy. They thought he was taking care of all of it. But really, he was orchestrating the whole thing. Smart, huh?"

"Didn't you just say... cops are stupid...?" Matt asks.

"Let me rephrase. Most cops," Oliver says cockily.

"Why gay kids?" I ask.

Brody smirks. "Because they are an abomination. Why do you think each victim was tattooed with the mark of the devil? I might have figured out a way to spare the two of you. Maybe skipped town. I have enough money from all the previous ransoms. I could disappear never to be seen again. But you had to turn out to be gay. Too bad. I liked the both of you."

Matt coughs again, spitting up more blood. "You'll never... get away with this." He's getting weaker and weaker. I can tell. I need to figure out how to get us out of here.

"There's so much shit that doesn't make sense, Brody. Your son. Isn't he gay?"

Oliver scoffs. "Fuck no. I only infiltrated the Order. I gained trust."

I nod. I had been right. "What about the banner?" I ask. "At the charity event? You intentionally put that the Order was working with GPD. Why?"

96

"Simple. To show you all how stupid you actually are," Oliver says. "But in hindsight, that may have been a little cocky of me."

"Why… are you doing this?" Matt asks.

Brody looks at him. "Do you know how much a Captain makes? Sending my son to school put me in an excessive amount of debt. His loans on top of mine? Fuck, I'll never pay that off."

"You won't get away with this," I growl low and dangerously. "No matter what happens to us. You'll never get away with this."

"Oh… I already have." Brody kneels in front of me. "But I'm willing to make you a deal. I'll let you live in exchange for your silence. But… you lose Matt."

I shake my head and look him straight in the eyes. "Fuck you." He pistol whips me with the butt of his gun, making a hard connection to the side of my head. I hit the ground hard, immediately seeing stars. I refuse to pass out. I groan and try to stay totally focused through the nausea and darkening vision. "Fuck…"

"I knew you'd say that." Brody reaches into his pocket and takes out his phone. He holds it out of my reach but shows me the screen.

I stop breathing. "No…" I meet Matt's eyes. Pain fills mine before I feel a very calm and cold sense of Alpha dominance and protection seep into my veins. My blood runs cold. I look at the picture once more as he takes it away and puts his phone back in his pocket. He still kneels next to me.

"So, you see. You'll do exactly what I say, DJ."

I glare up at him, feeling my cold blood turn hot and hum throughout my body. The picture is Layne with Lyric and Mariah. They are all wearing mouse ears in front of Hogwarts as the fireworks go off behind them.

"You won't touch my family," I growl dangerously. I punch up, connecting with his balls as hard as I possibly can. Brody's eyes roll, but he's in such an obvious amount of pain that he can't scream. Though, not for lack of trying. His mouth is open, but no sound comes out of it.

"Dad?" Oliver says in shock as he stares at his father. He levels the gun at me, but I'm faster. I move quickly. I wrap an arm around Brody's neck as I stand, using him as a shield. Oliver shoots, not being able to stop himself in time. Brody goes limp in my arms. Oliver's eyes widen in shock before he starts screaming. "Dad! Dad!"

I shove Brody into Oliver as he starts shooting again. Brody's body knocks Oliver to the ground as he screams animalistically. The gun is knocked out of his hand and skids across the floor towards Matt. Oliver shoves his father off him as I dive for the gun. Knowing Matt carries as well and that Oliver probably has his, I know I don't have time.

Just as Oliver comes up with Matt's gun, I grab mine. Oliver is still screaming hysterically as he points the gun at Matt. The basement door flies open. Oliver turns to the door just as a shot rings out. I shoot twice. One bullet hits his chest. The second connects with his head. Oliver falls backwards. Matt's gun clangs to the ground as I keep my gun pointed at Oliver with one eye on the door as I back up towards Matt.

"Check them!" Mariah yells pointing towards Brody and Oliver. I look up slightly confused as Mariah comes in with Lyric right behind her. Both are wearing bulletproof vests and leading an army of GPD's finest.

I turn to Matt and cup his cheek. His lip is split, and, like me, he looks worse for the wear. I kiss him softly and shakily. "Matt…"

"I'm okay. Sore. But okay." He kisses me back and buries his face in my neck when I hug him. "How about getting me the fuck out of these cuffs?"

"I got it," Lyric says as she uncuffs him.

His arms immediately wrap around me when he's free. He hugs me just as tightly as I am him. He kisses my neck. "I didn't see it coming. I'm sorry. So fucking sorry."

I pull away and run my thumb over his lip. "This isn't on you. We couldn't have predicted this. We knew we had a leak. We didn't know Oliver was Brody's son. We didn't know Brody was involved."

"I just don't get it. Why tell us the name? It was his son," Matt says.

"It was a trap," Lyric says. "Brody was at the party. He was waiting for the perfect moment. He knocked you both out."

"How did you two get here?" I ask, not willing to let Matt go.

"We saw Brody in Orlando. But he was hiding. He didn't know that we saw him. We checked into the hotel. We took an image of us all in bed. We checked in with you. We thought maybe he was tracking our phones and intercepting things. So we left our phones at the hotel. We took Layne and left. We brought him to the police station because we realized that Brody was the reason you two were so spooked and sent us away," Mariah explains.

"We knew as soon as we were off the grid, he'd follow. You both mentioned a party. So, when we got to the police station we called in a couple of guys from SWAT. We had them watch Layne locked in your office," Lyric says to Matt.

"Then we did a little bit of stealthy investigation on our own and found out where Brody was. We tapped into his squad's GPS. He was stupid enough to use the squad. The location was the address of the frat house. We got there too late," Mariah says. "But the president of the Order and Lang told us they were heading to the Science Building. Lang had lost track of Oliver."

"We found Brody's squad still sitting a couple of houses down. We called all squads, but had dispatch do it through their computers. We figured Brody would have a radio. We all met out back here because Lang and Andrew said that the murders had been taking place down here," Lyric continues.

"We would've been sooner, but we had to find someone who had access to the basement. We got the Dean down here, but we had to call the Chief to get the contact information. He wanted us to wait until he got here, but we heard the gunshots," Mariah finishes. "We were beyond terrified at what we'd find when we got in here."

I look up, not letting go of Matt, when I hear the Chief's voice booming in the basement. "What the hell is going on here?"

"We found the serial killer," I say as Matt burrows his head in my neck and hugs me tighter. I run my fingers through his hair.

"Explain to me why Captain Brody McKay is lying dead on the ground," he bellows.

I take a deep breath. "Brody was involved. Oliver was his son." I launch into the entire story, leaving nothing out. The Chief's face falls further and further. I gently sway with Matt and continue running my fingers through his hair.

Later, after we're all released from the scene, Matt and I crawl into bed. My bed. In my home. The sun is starting to rise. Lyric and Mariah are both in one of my guest rooms. Layne is safely tucked into his bed. For the first time since Matt and I have been together, he curls into me, laying his head on my chest.

99

"I love you, DJ," he whispers. "I've never been so fucking scared in my life. I woke up a few times while we were in that basement. The first time, I tried to get to you. I couldn't. You were just lying there. I thought you were dead. He hit me hard with the gun in the side of the head. Knocked me out. Every time I woke up, he was doing something to you. Kicking you. Hitting you. Pointing the gun at you. I couldn't get to you. Couldn't protect you. I thought we were going to die."

I kiss his head and run my hand up and down his arm. "But we didn't. We survived. We won. We saved countless lives. We saved my kids. We saved Mariah and Lyric. We saved our family."

He nods and actually burrows into me. Like he can't get close enough. "I know…"

I turn and hug him as closely as possible. I run my fingers through his hair and my hands up and down his back. I kiss his forehead and head. "I love you, too, Matt."

"Always and forever," he whispers as we both fall into an exhausted sleep we can't fight as all of the adrenaline coursing through us wears off.

"Always and forever," I whisper back before the sleep my body desperately needs overtakes me.

Epilogue

☆ Matt ☆

(Three Months Later)

I kiss the tip of DJ's nose just as Layne comes running into our bedroom. DJ smiles as he starts jumping up and down on the bed.

"Dads, come on. Breakfast. It's waiting."

I raise an eyebrow as he drops to his knees. "You made breakfast?"

"Yep! Destroyed the kitchen, too." He leaps off the bed and runs down the stairs.

"Fuck me. He's too hyper for this time of the morning," DJ grumbles as he gets up and heads for the bathroom.

I smile as I watch him. He's truly a beautiful man. He walks so gracefully. Every step he takes looks as dignified as it is calculated. I've honestly never seen another person look as perfect as him. Even when he's doing nothing but standing there, his muscles look like they're rippling.

"You coming in here with me? Or do you want me to beg?" he teases.

I briefly contemplate making him beg. But he looks far too enticing to put myself through the torture of waiting for him to do it. So instead, I stand and walk far too eagerly towards him as he disappears into the bathroom.

It's been a few months since we'd been undercover. It's taken us damn near that long to discover all of Brody's deceit. He'd covered so much evidence that it was truly amazing we were able to figure any of it out. His web was woven strongly. Breaking through took time and effort from almost the entire department.

By the time we had found the money he'd stolen and returned it to the families, we'd also discovered that he'd been living a complete double life. By day he was Brody McKay. Loving husband to a beautiful woman who couldn't conceive. Good cop. Respected member of the department and community.

By night, he was a disturbed man. Oliver had been his son, but his mother was a prostitute that Brody had raped numerous times and finally, maybe even mercifully, killed years ago. In fact, we'd found that he'd murdered several women over the years. But he'd made every single one of them look like overdoses. They were all prostitutes. He'd assigned himself the cases and closed them quickly. No one ever suspected anything more. We didn't have a reason to. His report matched that of the medical examiner. There was no evidence to suggest anything else.

We discovered that he'd only recently figured out Oliver was his son, but only after Oliver had searched him out. He never told his wife. His wife also didn't know that Brody was in deep with gambling debts. In fact, the bank was foreclosing on their home, and he'd left her with nothing. Given that she was a totally innocent victim in this entire thing, I'd allowed her to move into mine. She's renting it with an option to buy it if she chooses. I'd moved in with DJ almost right away because neither of us wanted to be apart any longer.

We'd also discovered that Oliver was, indeed, gay. He had joined the Order because he wanted a place where he could feel safe. It was just after he'd found his father. But Brody wasn't receptive in the slightest to his lifestyle. So, in order to please him, Oliver lied and said he'd infiltrated the Order to figure out how to destroy it from within. Brody couldn't have been more proud. What he didn't know was that Oliver really just wanted Andrew, his childhood friend and longtime crush. Interestingly enough, Andrew didn't remember him at all from when they were kids until we showed him pictures.

Turns out, Oliver was really Olivia. He'd gone through a sex change. By all appearances, not even Brody knew that. Oliver was in a lot of debt himself, not including college. Transgender surgery is not cheap and wasn't covered by the insurance that Oliver carried. The ransoms that the two of them took covered both Brody's debt and Oliver's secret debt.

The victims that Oliver chose all came from well-to-do families. He knew they'd do anything and pay anything to keep their kids safe. After they got the ransoms, they killed the victims. With Brody's help, the families were convinced to just pay with the promise that Brody would be able to track the money with a tracker that he told them he put in the bags with the money. It all happened very quickly, and what they didn't know was even though they'd paid, they would never see their kids again.

There were still a few things that we didn't know about the crimes. And without Brody or Oliver to tell us, we would probably never understand. One of those unknowns is how exactly he figured out where Mariah and Lyric had gone with Layne. We've found no evidence that Brody was working with anyone else in the department or anyone else at all.

After all was said and done, DJ and I had both been commended numerous times over. We have plaques and honors and commendations from the city, the department, the state, and even the LGBTQ community. We'd both become honorary members of Order of the Alpha Omega.

But the single thing that I am most proud of is DJ's promotion. With Brody's position vacated and no one in the position to fill it being willing to, DJ took the test with a couple of other lower ranked officers and another Sergeant. His results were off the charts. He was offered the Captain's position and accepted it with more enthusiasm than I've seen from him for a long time. I hadn't even known he wanted the promotion. He'd always told me he was happy right where he was. He'd never wanted a Lieutenant position when openings came. He was happy on the streets.

I shake the thoughts from my head as I close the bathroom door. When I turn back around, DJ is leaning against the counter watching me. He's completely naked. The shower is running. I make quick work of my boxers and walk towards him, wasting no time in crashing my lips to his.

He moans into the kiss and deepens it as he tangles his fingers in my hair. When he pulls away, he watches me a moment before running a thumb over my lower lip. "Where did you go on me? You got pretty lost in thought for a second."

I run my fingertips up his chest and shake my head. "I was thinking of everything that happened since we were undercover. It seems like everything has moved really fucking fast, but it seems perfect. Like this is how everything was meant to be. Us together. You as Captain. It just seems like everything has steadied out in both of our lives. Everything is just..." I smile and lean in to kiss him. "Perfect. It's perfect."

He smiles into the kiss before deepening it and backing us into the shower. I moan in pleasure when he grabs my dick and strokes at the same time the water hits us. He doesn't break the kiss or stop stroking as he closes the glass door to the shower.

Every hard ridge of his body is pressed against me when my back hits the shower wall, and he starts rotating his wrist as he strokes. I can only moan into his mouth in response and grip his shoulders as his tongue plunges into my mouth again and again in time to his strokes.

"Mmm... fuck you taste like everything I love," DJ says as he slowly stops stroking and turns me around. I reach behind me and grip his thighs as I press against the shower wall. I arch and moan when he slowly slides his dick deep in my ass. "And feel like every fucking wet dream I've ever had."

"Oh, fuck." My nails dig into his thighs as he starts thrusting. "Must have been some pretty good wet dreams."

"Like you haven't had some of your own." His teeth lightly scrape over my shoulder on the way to my neck.

I push back into him and tighten around him with each thrust as he kisses my neck. My dick gets harder and harder with each and every thrust until I have no choice but to let go of one of his thighs. I start stroking my dick in time to his thrusts.

"Oh, God, DJ." I drop my head back and turn. I nip at his neck as he thrusts harder and faster. Deeper. I match my strokes to his thrusts and moan and pant against him.

He turns and kisses me. I close my eyes and focus on how good he feels. His hands are all over me, sliding across my slick, solid abs. He wraps one arm around me as he deepens the kiss, tangling his tongue with mine once more. He pulls me into him as he thrusts. His other hand slowly trails down to my hard, throbbing dick.

He wraps his large hand around mine as I stroke. He nips my tongue as he smiles teasingly. "Need some help with that?"

"Fuck, yes."

DJ thrusts harder and deeper until he's buried balls deep in my ass. He's hit the perfect rhythm with his thrusts and strokes my dick with me at the same pace. I can feel his dick thicken as he moans and growls against my neck as he licks and kisses it. My dick starts jerking in our hands as the pressure builds.

"I'm gonna come," he whispers in my ear.

"Fuck," I whisper as I swallow. I clench my ass and tighten around him as he buries himself in me.

"Come with me."

I can do nothing more than nod. As soon as I feel him shoot his load deep in my ass, I come hard, shooting my own against the wall of the shower. "Holy shit, DJ."

"Fuck, Matt." He bites my shoulder lightly as he strokes me through and thrusts himself through the orgasm. His dick jerks in almost perfect harmony with mine as we come.

He keeps his hand over mine, gently squeezing my dick as he leans harder into me. He stays buried deeply in me as we both pant while we come down. I don't know when the water turned cold, but I don't care. He feels far too good to care about anything other than him.

After several moments he pulls out slowly and lets go of my dick as he kisses my shoulder and neck. "I'd like to do this all day, but... we have company coming soon."

I groan. "There are two people coming here that I'm okay with seeing. The rest of them, I could care less."

He laughs. "I know. But this is seriously the highlight of Lyric's year. Well, maybe after the part where she and Mariah knew how we were both pining for each other and threw it in our faces when we finally ended up together."

We clean up quickly and get dressed. A few minutes after we finish cleaning up the mess Layne made of the kitchen, Lyric and Mariah show up. I have no chance to react before Lyric bounces into the house and takes total control of everything. Including moving furniture so her decoration ideas can be created.

By the time she's done, DJ and I are staring both sweaty from moving things, and astounded at her blatant control. I look over at DJ. "Explain to me what just happened."

"What just happened? Lyric. The force that is Lyric. That. That is what just happened."

We both stare bewildered as she speeds around the house making last minute touches. Mariah quietly cooks all of the food and arranges it neatly on the counter. I'm fairly certain she hasn't said a single word the whole time she's been here. Just went quietly to work.

I look down at Lyric. She crinkles her nose as she looks up at us. "You both can't be the guests of honor looking and smelling like you came from the gym." She points to the stairs and says nothing more.

"We wouldn't if we hadn't had to rearrange my whole damn house," DJ says with a grin as we both head for our bedroom.

"Don't sass me, assholes. Shower. You reek."

We both know there's no point in arguing. Lyric might be a tiny girl, but fuck if either of us want to disobey her. She could probably destroy us both if she wanted to. I've seen the girl take down guys three times her size. Fucking with her? No thank you.

We both quickly clean up and change, then head back downstairs for what feels a little like a military inspection. Lyric stands looking at us with her hands behind her back. She keeps them there as she walks around us with her lips pursed as if she's deep in thought. She flicks something off my shoulder and runs her hand down DJ's ass like she's dusting something off.

DJ raises an eyebrow and looks back at her. "Not shy, are you?"

"Hush. You had fuzz on it." She walks back in front of us and nods. "Good. Perfect."

"We pass inspection, Ms. Sharpe?"

"Yes. You do. But…" She reaches up and smacks both of us in the back of the head.

"Ow!" I reach up and rub the back of my head, looking at her incredulously.

"What was that for?" DJ asks, rubbing the back of his. Mariah cracks up from the kitchen as we both watch Lyric.

Lyric puts her hands on her hips. "That? That was for being two big-headed asses and not telling the poor little women-folk everything that

106

was going on when you two were undercover. Just sending us away. We could've helped. And we could've been far better prepared to protect Layne." She smacks both of us hard on the arm.

"Hey!" I say shielding myself, defensively.

"Brat!" DJ says as he does the same.

I rub my arm. "Seriously? You honestly waited this long to do that?"

"I had to make sure you were both properly healed." She pouts. "Don't ever do that again. You both are the only family we have. Family sticks together."

DJ and I both look at each other before we bury her between us both in a giant hug. We kiss the top of her head as we feel her relax and hug us back.

"We're sorry," I say.

"We really didn't mean it like that. We were trying to protect you by keeping you out of it completely. We thought that was the best way to keep you both and Layne from being in danger. We didn't realize that he somehow knew to track you, or that he'd follow you," DJ says as he hugs her a little tighter.

"But we realize that it probably would have been far more beneficial if we'd let you in and told you what was happening. We promise we won't do anything like that again." I pull away slowly and hold up a pinkie, knowing what it means to Lyric.

She smiles brightly when she sees it and holds up her own, linking it with mine as she waits for DJ. DJ links his with us both.

Her smile grows mega-watt as she looks up at us. "Promise?"

"Promise." I lean down and kiss our linked pinkies.

DJ smiles and does the same. "Promise."

Mariah stealthily appears like a mini ninja and links her pinkie to ours. She kisses them just as Lyric leans in and kisses them as well. Together, they smile, and, in unison, say, "Promise!"

DJ nods and gives me a smirk as he lifts Lyric and throws her over his shoulder. Her eyes widen and she shrieks. "DJ! Don't you dare! Mariah! Help!"

Mariah starts after them, but I catch her around the waste and throw her over my shoulder. She screams and squirms. "Matthew! Don't you fucking dare!"

I slap her ass at the same time DJ slaps Lyrics. Before either of them can do anything to retaliate, we throw them into the pool. They scream as we both crack up. When they come to the surface, though, we both shut our mouths. They look a little like the twins from Stephen King's *The Shining*. We both take an involuntary step back as we watch them.

They look at each other as they spit water out of their mouths and push their long hair out of their face. They both glare as they pull themselves out of the pool. Lyric looks up at us as she rings out her hair.

"You are going to pay for that," she growls.

"Looking forward to it," DJ pushes.

I elbow him. "There's a change of clothes for you both in the guest room."

"Oh we know," Mariah says.

They both go in to change as guests start to arrive at the party DJ and I aren't entirely certain we really want. But it's to celebrate his promotion. A little bit of a coming out party as well, because we have no intention of hiding. If I feel like kissing my boyfriend, I'm going to.

The party goes long into the night with no retaliation from the girls. Which makes me suspicious as fuck. I've been watching them all day and night, though, and they've seemingly forgotten everything. In fact, they're turning up the cute couple vibes and making everyone around them wish they could have a relationship like them.

But I know better. I know they can hold a grudge for as long as they want to until they see an opening for revenge. Mariah and Lyric are two women I'd never want to get on the bad side of. I send sympathy to anyone who does.

DJ snuggles into my side and hides a yawn. "We need to make everyone go away. A ten hour party is too long, and Layne needs to go to bed."

"On it, baby." I turn and kiss him deeply.

And it's then that they take their revenge. I feel the push and can't correct it as DJ and I go sailing into the pool. We go under, fully-clothed and still holding each other while looking at each other with the amount of shock someone would feel when they see they won a million dollars.

When we resurface, Lyric and Mariah are hugging each other and laughing. We pull ourselves out of the pool as they run away. Everyone is laughing. DJ and I join in the laughter as we walk towards the house.

When we're almost near the door, a giant cloud of glitter decorated confetti surrounds us.

Pink.

Glitter.

Confetti.

We both turn slowly around and see Layne holding a giant bucket with the remnants of glitter confetti in it. We look down at everything sticking to us before looking back up at Layne. Lyric and Mariah come up behind them.

"That… was…" I shake my head trying to be mad, but it's impossible. DJ and I both crack up. Layne runs to Mariah and Lyric laughing as if they'll protect him or something.

"Game on, son," I say with a teasing glare.

I don't know what the future has in store for us, but I do know that what we have, all of it, is everything I've ever wanted. For the first time in my life, I can honestly say I'm happy. And I can feel DJ is, too.

We're surrounded by love.

Contentment.

Being who we truly are. Finally. After so long.

It feels like we're finally whole. Complete.

Free.

The End

Next In The Beautiful Dream Series

The sweet and sinfully sexy Beautiful Dream Series continues with
Captain Charming.

Given my ladies' man reputation, most people wouldn't think of me as romantic. I'm tough. I can be gruff. A hard ass. I know being a Captain with the Gainesville Police Department has probably gotten me more than a few dates.

Truthfully, all I've ever wanted is to settle down. I've just never found the right woman to do it with.

Until Mariah Marie comes into my life.

She's enchanting. Beautiful. Sweet. Intelligent. Fierce. She has a wicked sense of humor, and a tantalizing way with words.

Her popularity as a romance author has grown exponentially in a very short period of time. Wherever she graces with her presence, a call for service is sure to follow. Calls I usually assign myself to. I don't trust anyone else to keep the girl I'm falling in love with safe.

When the innocent adoration of one of her fans becomes sinister, I'll do whatever it takes to protect my girl. Suddenly, we're both thrust into a dangerous world that threatens to destroy us.

A world I don't know either of us will make it out of alive.

Order *Captain Charming* Today!

The Beautiful Dream Series

Available Now

Loving You
My Love, My Heart
Softening Lyric
Undercover Temptations
Captain Charming
Breaking Boundaries
Crashing Into You
Tactical Inferno
Ravishing Our Queen
Cherished By The Texan
Unveiling Our Passions

Box Sets Available

The Beautiful Dream Series: Box Set: Part 1
The Beautiful Dream Series: Box Set: Part 2

Other Books By Melony Ann
The Crane Family Series

Available Now

The Reluctant Mafia King
Sweet Lies
Billion Dollar Love Story
Be Mine
Protecting Her
Dangerously Forbidden Love
His Heart
Love In The Dark

Box Sets Available

The Crane Family Series

The Deimos Trilogy

Available Now

Connor's Legacy
Aryan's Alpha
Kade's Redemption

Box Sets Available

The Deimos Trilogy

The Forbidden Temptation Series

Available Now

The Detective's Forbidden Temptation
The Running Back's Forbidden Temptation

The Lucinio Family Series

Available Now

Rising From The Ashes
The Player's Rebel
Encrypting My Heart
Fighting My Fate

Multi Author Series
Piper Falls: Firehouse 49

Available Now

Ignite My Fire by Melony Ann
Regain My Fire by Kindra White
Playing With My Fire by D.L. Howe
Fight My Fire by Darley Collins
Against My Fire by Anneke Boshoff
Relight My Fire by Louise Murchie
Harness My Fire by Ayana Lisbet
Quench My Fire by Havana Wilder

Let's Be Friends

Follow me on

Bookbub

Facebook

Goodreads

Instagram

Tik Tok

Visit my website
www.melonyannauthor.com

Subscribe to my newsletter and get a FREE never-seen-before NOVELLA
just for subscribers!
https://www.melonyannauthor.com/exclusive-content

Join my Facebook Reader Group!
Melony Ann's Sizzling Book Nook
https://www.facebook.com/groups/melonyannssizzlingbooknook

The official Beautiful Dream Series Playlist on YouTube
https://youtube.com/playlist?list=PLGEiD5wbQmDe1z4_FeeKbMLcBkOz
1M4L4

Dedication

To our always and forever.

Acknowledgements

Weston and Henry - You aren't supposed to be reading these books... But... I know you do. So..., I wanted to say that this book is dedicated to you. I want you to know that your sexuality is no one's business but your own. You need to be happy and content in your own skin. If that means you are attracted to girls, that's okay. If you're attracted to guys, that's also okay. And if you're attracted to both guys and girls, there is nothing wrong with that. It took me YEARS to come to terms with my own sexuality. So many people, including my own father, made me feel like being a lesbian, gay, bi-sexual, pansexual, or anything other than straight was wrong. But it's not. There is nothing wrong with me. Just like there is nothing, let me repeat that, NOTHING wrong with you. You're young. You have so much time to decide who you are. But, truthfully, you're a lot like me. You know who you are. And again, it's okay. So, this book is for you. Because it's really all about two guys coming into their own sexuality. Figuring out who they really are and owning it. Finally deciding that who they are is okay. No one can change it. No one can take it away. And while you have so much time to really decide who you are and what you like, you should never ever hide who you are. I love you, Little Alpha. And know you have your whole family behind you and an entire army of people supporting you. We all love you.

Brad - I'm starting to run out of creative ways to say I love you. But I do love you. More and more every day, Beta.

Laura - I still can't believe how lucky I am and how much I've fallen for you over these last months. You're so amazing, creative, and talented. I'm so proud of all you've accomplished. I love you so much, Little Luna.

Jay - You know when you feel like everything is perfect in life? And then something happens and you realize that you never knew what perfect was until just that very moment? Well, that's how everything is with you. Everything was perfect. Right. And then you came along and showed us all what perfect really is. And here I am falling more and more in love with you, trying to figure out exactly how it all happened. But I wouldn't change a moment. I love you, Alpha.

Anneke – I'm not entirely certain this book would have come to be if not for you pushing me to just make it happen. Thanks for those chats.

Jason – We went to hell, but we never came back.

Kayla – I'm 100% positive that I would be somewhere in a dark hole right now if not for you. Things are an unbelievable ball of fucked up. Thanks for being here for me.

To the Bookstagram Community.

To my family.

To all of those who believe in me and support me.

To all of those who don't.

Cover by: Carter Cover Designs

Edited by: Alyssa Skaggs

About Melony Ann

Melony Ann began writing short stories and poetry as a child. She continued honing her craft over the years until she took the plunge and began publishing her work, despite having severe anxiety.

Melony writes contemporary romance stories that are full of suspense and a lot of steam.

When she isn't writing, she is loving her family and working to make her life something she deserves.

Melony believes that if her writing can inspire just one person, then all of her hard work is worth it.

Her hope is that her writing allows each and every one of her readers to escape for a little while. To dive into a different world one book at a time.

www.ingramcontent.com/pod-product-compliance
Lightning Source LLC
Chambersburg PA
CBHW050738230626
47052CB00003BA/517